SINGLE, SAVED, SEARCHING

A TRUE LOVE NOVELLA

Books by Renée Allen McCoy

From The True Love Novellas Series
The Christmas Beau
Single, Saved, & Searching
A Test of Faith (Forthcoming title)

The Fiery Furnace Series
The Kiss of Judas
Confessions
The Eleventh Hour

Stand-Alone Title
In the Presence of My Enemies

Non-fiction
Soul Ties: Breaking Up with a Past That's Killing Your Future

Short Story
Once Upon a Sunday

SINGLE, SAVED, & SEARCHING

A TRUE LOVE NOVELLA

Renée Allen McCoy

FaytheWorks Publishing

FaytheWorks Publishing, LLC
Faith works together in Christ.

Brandon, MS 39047
mail@faytheworks.com

Single, Saved, & Searching
© 2014 by Renée Allen McCoy

This book is a work of fiction. Names, characters, places (specifically noted: Lewiston Springs, MS) and incidents are either products of the author's creativity or used fictitiously. Any resemblance to actual events or locales or persons, living or dead, is entirely coincidental with the exception of God, Jesus Christ, and the Holy Spirit: They are real. Although this body of work is fictional, The Holy Trinity is not.

ISBN-10: 0-9836046-5-7
ISBN-13: 9780983604655

Library of Congress Control Number: 2014922096

Acknowledgments

Father, I thank You for all of Your many blessings ... I couldn't possibly name them all. I thank You for Your Son, my Lord and Savior Jesus Christ, and for Your Holy Spirit, my Comforter and Guide. Through You I am blessed and highly favored. Although I had stopped writing for five years some time ago, You still kept this gift inside of me to use for Your Kingdom. To You, I give all the honor, glory, and praise, knowing that without You I can do nothing, but with You all things are possible.

To my family, friends, and readers thank you so much for the love and support shown. It warms my heart to know that there are genuine people in my corner, rooting me on. I pray that you all are greatly blessed by God. Whatever He has placed inside of you to share with the world, know that He'll give you confirmation to know that it is truly from Him.

Single, Saved, & Searching is my seventh book to date. In writing it, I was reminded of what it was like to be single and waiting. In that time before marriage, God taught me that I had to be the kind of person I wanted to marry. In a nutshell, if you desire a strong, vibrant, God-fearing spouse, be sure that you are that too, and don't settle.

Roughly three years before I met my husband and was married, I told someone the kind of spouse I wanted. In response, this friend said that I was not going to find that kind of person. And she went on to tell me her reasoning why. I thought for a moment to myself and dismissed that idea, and instead chose to believe that he was out there. God said that He would give me the desires of my heart, and He did. Listen to God's word over the words of people. He knows best.

And my speech and my preaching were not with persuasive words of human wisdom, but in demonstration of the Spirit and of power, that your faith should not be in the wisdom of men but in the power of God (1 Corinthians 2:4-5).

I hope you enjoy this second installment of The True Love Novellas: *Single, Saved, & Searching.*

The Bible is still the greatest story ever told.

In His Name,
Renée Allen McCoy

He who finds a wife finds a good thing,
and obtains favor from the Lord.
~Proverbs 18:22

Chapter One

Strong, black, educated, and responsible—those are the characteristics Elisha would love to have in man, to name a few. Blinded to the world's standard of beauty, he'd be resourceful enough to create his own. Stand as a model of independence, an example of strength, an advocate of loyalty, and a pillar of integrity.

As she stared at her boyfriend through squinted eyes, Elisha wondered if she was asking for too much. Her friend Gina had told her yes while her other friend, Tonia, had emphatically declared no. Caught up somewhere in the middle Elisha wondered, *what does my man say?* After a dismissive grunt, she knew that he'd say he possessed all of those qualities and then some. But in her eyes, that was far from the truth.

Chauncey McDaniel was strong in the sense that he bench pressed more than her and one of her girlfriend's weight, but when it came to knowing God's Word and standing up for Biblical principles, he fell short. He certainly was black, as dark as they came, but not as educated as she would like and certainly not responsible enough to introduce him to her parents. Chauncey's family was rich and he pretty much had everything handed to him, but the wealth still didn't comfort Elisha enough to completely abandon her values.

"Why are you so quiet?" Elisha asked, noticing that Chauncey hadn't spoken three words to her since they got inside of one of his prized possessions, a red convertible Porsche 911 Carrera Cabriolet. "Did you have too much to drink?"

"If I had too much to drink, would you be on the passenger side? Don't say stupid things that don't make sense." He callously shook his head.

"I don't even know why I'm with you. All of sudden you're a drunk. You never drank when we first started dating." Elisha sucked her teeth. "Leave it up to you to ruin a perfectly good evening." She cut her eyes away from him and with folded arms sunk down into the soft leather-trimmed, heated seat.

Chauncey grunted under his breath and then tightened his lips again. Soon, he took the last busy street before the secluded, residential road where Elisha lived. After he parked in front of her garage, the neighbors who lived next door were just pulling out of their driveway. Chauncey casually waved as did Elisha before the neighbors disappeared out of sight. Chauncey then carefully looked at the darkened house across the street that shared the wooded dead end as Elisha's home.

"Are they out of town again?" he questioned, as they stood at the front of his car.

Elisha glanced back and then remembered, "Oh yeah, I told them that I'd turn the lights on for them tonight." She reached inside of her handbag and began fidgeting with the keys on her ring, and then started down her driveway.

Chauncey grabbed her by the arm and yanked her back. "That can wait." The force in his voice was tighter than the grip on her arm. "I told you that we'd talk at home."

With slightly parted lips, Elisha's gaze on him drifted down to the hand he held her with.

"Now get inside." His voice demonized as he commanded, snatching her towards the front steps. Chauncey looked back one last time before he slammed the door behind them.

Anger and rage filled his eyes like never before. Elisha watched in horror as the man who claimed to love her gritted his clenched teeth. Their eyes met as she edged backwards into the kitchen. Chauncey noticed her subtle movements and pounced on her like she was defenseless prey. He struck her face with a sudden back hand slap and Elisha's slender body went soaring through the air. She slammed against the door of the stainless steel refrigerator, and then dropped to the floor.

Slow to move, Elisha grimaced as she braced her arched back with one hand while covering her cheek with the other. After several laboring breaths, she struggled to push her body up before meeting eyes with Chauncey who glared at her.

"Get out!" she screamed through heavy pants. "Just get out of my house!"

Her words only fueled his anger. No woman, especially one that he claimed to be his own, was going to disrespect him in front of his friends and get away with it. Especially the friends he always tried to impress. The way everyone laughed when Elisha made a crack about him being a mama's boy drove Chauncey insane. Stone-faced practically the rest of the evening out as everyone shared funny and embarrassing stories over dinner, Chauncey stewed as he waited for the precise moment to teach his girlfriend a lesson.

"Shut up!" he shouted, and then kicked her in the stomach with his Prada round toe boots. Despite her raspy coughs, Chauncey continued pounding on her.

After yanking her up by the cashmere sweater she wore, he punched her in the head and shoved her back to the floor. Elisha's hair swung from its sleek do to a disheveled mess. Strands fell forward and covered her face.

"Maybe that'll teach you that my business with my mother is *my* business." His eyebrows furrowed, further emphasizing his point. "Learn how to keep your mouth shut!" He pointed at her in disgust, oblivious of the blood that oozed from her face. "And don't think I didn't see you flirting with Vic. Yeah, I never really thought he was just a *family friend*."

In a state of disorientation, Elisha's voice quivered, "*Oh God…*" just above a whisper as pain rippled through her body.

"I said shut up!" Chauncey snarled.

Knowing her strength was no match for his, Elisha cowered on the floor, curled in a fetal position. The entire time they had been together, she never even entertained the idea of being with another man. She listened as Chauncey spun through the kitchen like an angry tornado, sweeping envelopes, papers, ceramic vases, and everything else in his path of destruction onto the floor all the while ranting about how she didn't respect him as a man. When she caught a glimpse of her stainless steel letter opener among the debris scattered across the floor, Elisha inched toward it.

"Just look at what you made me do." Chauncey stared back at her and she froze. "For over a year I've been there for you," he justified. "I guess the trips to Costa Rica, Venezuela, and Panama meant nothing to you. Not to mention that diamond necklace I got you for Valentine's yesterday."

The heart-shaped pendant that dangled from Elisha's necklace no more showed the love he said he had for her than the fist he used to pound her.

"I try to show you how much I care, but then you go and say stupid stuff in front of people like you're trying to embarrass me or something." His voice deepened to a mocking tone as he asked, "Who's embarrassed now? See how many men would drop the kind of change on you that I have."

Elisha struggled to fight back the tears that had formed in her heart a long time ago behind this man. After all that had happened between them over the past year, she desired an honest effort from him instead of empty promises. That was until tonight. Their break-ups were old and anybody that knew them never believed that they belonged together in the first place.

Chauncey's smile lured Elisha into his world, and his boyish good looks kept her there. It baffled her how he managed to finagle her into a relationship with him when he was no more saved than his playboy father she had met when they visited him in California a few months prior. *Maybe it was his money*, she remorsefully reasoned. As a saved woman, she had been praying for the past year that Chauncey would give his life to Christ. But after numerous visits to her church and no commitment to the Lord, Elisha wondered if he would ever love God as she does. Tonia would always say to her, "You can't be his girl and his savior. He's got to know God for himself. Just let God do His job."

As Chauncey paced back and forth in front of Elisha, he inadvertently kicked the letter opener out of her reach. Elisha closed her eyes in defeat and tears dripped to the floor. It was at that moment she realized that God had spared his life because the rage and fear bubbling inside of her was strong enough to kill him. Especially after the way he had just beaten her and damaged some of the things she cherished so dearly.

The kitchen that had been beautifully decorated by her mother was a complete mess. The rare, fragile artifacts bought overseas by her father were broken into jagged pieces on the hardwood floor. He not only wanted to ruin her physically, but destroy her emotionally as well.

"I love you, Elisha. You just make me crazy some-times," he growled in a deranged tone. "I want things to work between us. You know that I love you, right?"

Afraid to even make eye-contact with him, Elisha's double vision merged back into one. She kept her head low and face toward the floor. She soon realized that he was not only delusional to think she would go back to him, but psychotic.

Chauncey knelt on the floor and touched Elisha's arm. She glared up at him and instinctively snatched away. His eyes widened when he saw the blood on her face. He almost couldn't stand to look at what he had done. "Oh Elisha … I-I'm sorry."

Her lips quivered uncontrollably.

"I don't know what came over me," Chauncey dared to explain.

Elisha smeared aside strands of her hair that was matted to her bloody face.

Chauncey turned his head, avoiding eye contact as he said, "So, I guess you're going to tell your mother now." He fretfully sighed, knowing his fate if she did. "Please don't," he shamelessly begged, looking back to her. "I promise … it'll never happen again. Trust me, I love you. Nobody will ever love you like me. I-I'm sorry, baby. I'll do whatever you want me to."

Elisha mustered up the strength to scream, "Just leave!"

Chauncey heard the seriousness in her voice and saw the hurt in her eyes. Afraid that she would call the police, he fled through the front door in a panic. Moments later, Elisha was left alone with her wounds.

Images flashed through her head of when he had slapped her months ago. Tonia, the only friend who knew about the assault, told her that it wouldn't be the last time he put his hands on her. After tonight, Elisha found out that was true. She never thought that it would have gone this far, especially over something so incredibly stupid. Tonia had also told her to let the loser go because if she had to mold him into what she wanted, there was a good chance that he would end up molding her into someone she didn't want to be. She was right about that too.

Elisha dragged herself to her purse a few feet away and grabbed the cell from the side panel. She blankly stared at the lighted screen which displayed the numbers 911. The longer she stared, the more she thought about what other people would say about her. She didn't want to be called stupid or crazy for staying with a man that had hit her before. Although her mother, a licensed attorney, could put him behind bars for what had happened to her tonight, she promised that this would be her secret.

Elisha trembled as she remembered what her parents had always told her, "Love does not hurt." Shame filled her teary eyes as she stared at her blurred reflection in the bathroom mirror. She gazed down at the trail of blood that had followed her to the porcelain sink and soon her quiet sniffles turned into uncontrollable sobs. At that life-changing moment, Elisha vowed to never let another man beat on her again.

Never.

Chapter Two

One year later...

Love was in the air, but Elisha Maxwell still felt all alone. She flipped the pages of her desk calendar back from February to December of the previous year and stared at the date she knew her sister, Charity, had realized the love of her life. It was at the Christmas gala their mother had hosted where Charity and an old boyfriend of hers, Milton, had starred in a play together. The kind of love Elisha saw that Milton had for Charity was the kind of love she wanted in her own life.

Elisha sat slumped with the sides of her face pressed into the palms of her hands and gently sighed. It had been an incredibly tough work week for her that led up to Valentine's Day—a day she had been dreading ever since her assault from last year. She was resolved to move on, so this day was particularly hard since the new guy she had her eye on asked another woman to marry him. When Elisha met Will it had already been eight months since she had seen the likes of her abusive ex, Chauncey McDaniel. She later learned that he had left town just a day after he beat her up and knowing that he was gone gave her the relief she needed to finally move on.

Elisha replayed in her mind the conversations she and Will had that all but sealed the notion he was single. Not once did he mention that he was attached, spoken for, or in any kind of committed relationship. This man had quietly wooed her, to say the least, sharing details about his future plans when they met for the first time at the state fair last fall, calling during the holidays to bid her a Happy Thanksgiving and Merry Christmas, in addition to texting her a beautiful salutation on New Year's Eve. They had several out-of-town dates between the counties in which they lived where he surprised her with thoughtful gifts. She was careful though to wait until he confirmed their relationship status before announcing it to family and friends. Just when she thought he was going to officially ask her to be his woman a few weeks ago, Will told Elisha he was getting married.

Married? Elisha grunted as she remembered how she was beginning to fall for him. He had been the closest she had come to being in a decent relationship in a long time. In an attempt to clear Will from her mind, she spun the pages of her desk calendar back to February and powered down her computer.

She bowed her head with elbows propped on her desk and prayed to God. Elisha prayed specifically for the Lord to send her a mate—*her soul mate*. She had always figured that God knew what she wanted, and He does, but there was something about *asking* Him specifically for the desires of her heart. And today her heart was set on getting married. There wasn't a boyfriend in sight, but Elisha trusted God to know what was best for her. All she had to do was listen for and to His answer.

On this Friday afternoon, she tidied her desk in preparation to leave for the lovers' weekend; the weekend that held nothing special for her except a marathon of television movies and bad memories of what had happened to her a year ago. As principal of the elementary school she once attended as a child, she enjoyed being at work, but the fact that every female in her office received decorative balloons, endearing cards, soft teddy bears, and special deliveries while she got nothing only made her want to leave work early.

"Are you leaving already?" Jasmine, the administrative assistant, asked Elisha as she emerged from her office.

"Uh, yes. I'm taking off an hour early today." Elisha slowly nodded as she adjusted the three quarter length, beige coat that was draped across her arm. "So, if anything comes up, you can still reach me on my cell." She closed her office door behind her.

"Oh, okay. Well, you have a good weekend," Jasmine answered with a smile as her eyes drifted to the lovely bouquet of roses on her desk accompanied by a red heart-shaped box of milk chocolates. "I know I will," she modestly added with a smile.

"See you next week." With a quiet exhale, Elisha shifted her eyes away from Jasmine's gifts and blankly stared at the large colorful arrangement of balloons floating between her and the exit.

"Oh, I'm so sorry, Ms. Maxwell." Jasmine rustled up the assortment of balloons and wrapped the attached coiled strings that hung from them around her hand, clearing the preoccupation from Elisha's face. "This was a delivery for one of the teachers. She was supposed to come and get them during her free period. Since I have a minute, I'll just take them to her."

Elisha watched as Jasmine maneuvered the balloons out into the hallway and within seconds disappeared from view. With a depressive gaze, Elisha waved goodbye to the data specialist who was on the phone. She quietly slipped inside of her coat and headed for the parking lot. Moments later her mind ran on Will again, the man whom she thought would have been hers.

As Elisha remembered the times they talked over the phone and occasionally met for coffee during the few short months she had known him, she wondered why he never mentioned being in a relationship. In hindsight, she figured that maybe she read too much into their casual acquaintanceship, desperately wanting the longstanding relationships that many of her close friends had, namely her sister, Charity, who was recently engaged. She figured that it was either that or she was still trying to get over that terrible relationship she had ended with

Chauncey last year. The bruises on her body had healed beautifully, but the ones on her heart were still raw.

"Oh my goodness, I'm so sorry," Elisha apologized profusely. She was so consumed with the idea of finding that special someone, that she didn't see the person in front of her.

The tall, dark stranger held up a hand as a gesture to accept her apology for accidentally knocking the candy Fabergé eggs from his hands to the ground. "It's okay," he said, examining the elegantly decorated eggs inside of its semi-transparent carton for cracks. "It's packaged pretty well."

"Are you sure?" Elisha's eyes widened, still staring down at the colorful package. "I'll pay for it," she graciously offered.

The attractive man looked up from the candy, having recognized her voice. "Elisha?"

As Elisha looked up from his large hands beyond the charismatic smile on his face to his piercing brown eyes, a flood of familiar emotions seized her attention. As she watched the corners of his mouth rise, Elisha couldn't believe that it was him. He had grown a mustache and a well-trimmed beard that altered his already distinct look. Years after not speaking to one another following his acquittal of a trumped up aggravated assault charge, Elisha's feet were frozen in place.

"*Man*, you still look good." His eyes roamed from her bewildered expression to the hand firmly planted on her stomach.

"Ty—Tyler?" she slowly stammered, glancing at a passerby before shifting her attention back to him. "Uh, how have you been?" Elisha's eyes drifted from Tyler's handsome face to his broad shoulders. The leather jacket he wore hung slightly open revealing the wool blend sweater that rested easily against his flat abdomen. He had kept himself in shape to the point where it caused her to take a second glance.

Tyler slowly moistened his lips while gently shaking his head. "It's okay, Elisha. I know what the word is around town." He watched as she nervously rubbed the nape of her neck. "Look, I'm not going to hold you up. It was good seeing you, though." His eyes drifted from hers to the ground.

Elisha sighed heavily as Tyler walked around her and towards the school. Several seconds later, she called out to him, "Tyler, wait."

Tyler's feet trudged to a stop and faced the woman who used to be his best friend. They used to be able to tell each other anything until he was accused of the unthinkable. He had understood her anger, for a moment in time, but it shocked him when she refused to hear his side of the story.

"I'm sorry that I didn't answer any of your calls," she confessed.

Tyler took a few steps back in her direction with the candy gift for his mother securely tucked under his arm. "Are you really? Because the way I hear it is that you're sorry you ever trusted me to be in your life."

Elisha defensively propped a hand on her hip and pointed at him with the other. "Don't go there. You know that's not true."

"Well, you sure didn't convey that to your DA mother."

Elisha paused, and then rolled her eyes upward. She looked back at him and shook her head. "My mother was just doing her job. What did that have to do with me?"

"For starters, you knew where I was that night—"

"*No*," she interrupted. "I knew where you were that day."

"But Elisha, you never asked me if I did it." He patted a hand on his chest. "You knew that I would never beat on a woman," Tyler's voice lowered as he continued, "let alone rape her. You know me better than that."

Elisha's long eyelashes fluttered as she swiped a section of her silky, black hair behind her ear. "Well, sometimes people do things you never thought they'd do."

"Seriously?" he questioned, taking another step in her direction. "So, you put me in that category? Elisha, I thought we were better than that."

"We were," she sternly answered with a raised eye-brow. "I don't know what we are now." Elisha tightened the coat belt around her waist.

Tyler stared at her with countless questions in his eyes, well aware that his lifelong friendship with Elisha was never going to be the same after the vicious accusations swarmed around town. When the case was a hot topic, her mother was the DA and he was easily branded as a dirty cop, a label that would have been hard to live down in a town where everybody knew everybody. After the acquittal, Tyler left the state and started over in the neighboring state of Tennessee. The only thing that kept bringing him back home was to visit his mother, a seasoned teacher at the elementary school, and the hope of getting the one woman he wanted to take with him when he had left.

"Well, I know you. If you really thought I was the monster your mother made me out to be, you wouldn't be standing here talking to me now. Or is it like mother, like daughter these days?" His words, although brutally honest, carried along with them the hint of a smile that gradually drew one out of her too.

"Tyler, you don't know what you're talking about." She curled her lightly glossed lips and rolled her chestnut colored eyes.

"I know how much her opinion matters to you." Tyler quickly became serious again. "She practically ran your life."

"You really think you still know me after all of these years?" Elisha casually folded her arms across her chest in a way that challenged him to answer otherwise. "My mother does not run my life." She shook her head as if to convince even herself. "She never did."

"Prove it," he dared her.

"What do you mean *prove it*?"

"Let's hang out."

"Hang out? What are we, sixteen years old now?" she teased.

"Whatever, you know what I mean. Let's get together like we used to. Comedy club, dinner, games," he paused as she giggled, "the whole nine. Prove to me that you know who I am despite what was said about me in that courtroom over two years ago."

Elisha's giggles faded as she heard the seriousness in Tyler's voice and gazed into his eyes. At that moment, she saw something different in them. She had missed their friendship too, and although she refused to admit that he was right, Margaret's opinion did weigh heavily in her life. It was clearly evident when she had the opportunity to put Chauncey behind bars and didn't. Instead of making her private life public, Elisha kept the assault a secret to avoid hearing the redundant play of the words *I told you so* from not only her mother, but her friends as well.

After she took two weeks off from work last year where everyone thought she was on vacation, Elisha left town and took the time to heal. When questioned about what had become faint discolorations on her skin that makeup couldn't cover by the time she returned, she simply brushed it off by describing it as a hard fall.

"So, can you prove it?" Tyler repeated in a patronizing tone. "I'm in town for a couple of weeks."

"Oh yeah, that's right. Your mother is having surgery on Monday," she recalled, remembering the leave slip Ms. Hampton had previously submitted.

"Yeah, so, what do you say?" Tyler steered her back to their original conversation. "I mean, that's if you don't have a date or something." His smile was priceless.

"It's Valentine's weekend," she responded in a defensive tone. "Have you ever known me to not have a date?"

Tyler stared at her sideways, knowing her at times better than she knew herself, and said, "So this means you don't."

Elisha's response stalled, and then she cracked a smile. "Okay, no, no I don't. But I could have. I know I still got it." She put a hand on her hip again.

"Elisha, you always did," he admitted, and then laughed along with her.

With a playful roll of her eyes, Elisha grinned. Despite the time they'd spent apart, Tyler was still the only man that she could tell almost anything. *Almost*. They had been best friends since elementary school having met nearly twenty-five years ago just steps away from where they now stood.

"Okay, deal," Elisha agreed.

"Okay?" he skeptically questioned.

"Yeah … okay. Just call me after you've seen your mother. The cell number is the same."

"I still got it."

"I kind of figured that," she quipped, and then pulled her keys from the side pocket of her satchel. "I'll text you directions to my house." Before Elisha turned to walk away, she added with a smirk, "And dinner is on you."

"You wouldn't have it any other way." Tyler grinned, remembering how she always used to make him pay for dinner even though they had never been a couple. "No problem, seafood it is." He winked. "The fish house is on the way to my mother's house. I'll just cook that dish you like for old time's sake. Grilled salmon, yellow rice, and steamed asparagus. I got you. I remember what you always used to say. You're just not a catfish kind of girl."

Elisha smirked at his comment and then opened her car door. As Tyler proceeded to the school's front entrance, she was pleasantly surprised that after years of not seeing one another he still remembered her favorite meal.

Chapter Three

She's getting married, too? Elisha sighed as she dropped the engraved invitation onto her granite counter next to the one she had received from her sister, Charity, just two days prior.

Jaleesa, a friend from college, had sent her a text several months ago that she had a new boyfriend. It was around the same time Elisha and Will were dating. Or what she thought could have been described as dating. Elisha figured that it would have been something if they both found their soul mates before the age of thirty since their other close friends, Tonia and Gina, had both been married for three and four years, respectively.

The fact that her last single girlfriend and younger sister were both celebrating their upcoming nuptials caused her otherwise cheerful mood to sour upon hearing the news. Charity was marrying Milton Grayson, a friend and former classmate of Elisha's, and Jaleesa was marrying someone she described as the love of her life. As Elisha stared back at the lovely shade of peach and silver engraved design, her eyes clouded with tears. It was all she could do as she remembered the relationships she had been in and out of over the past few years.

The ringing phone snapped her from the daze, but she fought to shake the pity party she was about to throw for herself. No matter how attractive men said she was or how many hours she spent working out, Elisha still felt insecure.

"Hey," she answered her cell. "No, no, I just got home." She cleared her throat while wiping the tears from beneath her eyes. "No, I actually have plans," Elisha explained to Tonia as she moved about the kitchen, preparing for a friendly evening with Tyler. She placed the phone on speaker and grabbed two new placemats from the baker's rack next to the patio door.

"Plans?" Tonia said in a tone that caused Elisha to chuckle.

"Uh, yes. It is Valentine's weekend, you know," Elisha responded in a condescending tone. "Or have you forgotten to take a date break since you had that kid of yours?"

This time Tonia giggled. "That *kid*, as you put it, has a name. Not to mention that she's your Godchild. Besides, where am I going to go in this cold weather with a six-week-old baby?"

"Hey, you're the one who used to be everywhere when you were pregnant. I'm still trying to get over you showing up at the gala my mom had around Christmas."

"Well, you know, everybody was home and it was good to see Milton and Charity together again."

Elisha melted at the thought that her little sister had found true love. Despite the tension that threatened to tear them apart, she was genuinely happy to see them together again. When Milton asked Charity to marry him on stage after the standing ovation they had received for the play they had just performed, it was a storybook ending.

"Yeah, it was ... and is. I just got her invitation in the mail a couple days ago." Elisha paused as she picked up her sister's wedding invitation again. "They're not wasting any time."

"Oh, what's the date?" Tonia inquired with her voice full of anticipation. She had been wearing elastic maternity clothes for the longest and longed for an event where she could dress up and look like her old self again.

"April," Elisha flatly replied. "Can you believe it?"

"Hey, when it's right, it's right." Tonia chuckled. "I mean, why wait?"

Elisha's sentiments were the same. It just seemed that her relationships were never right. She's never felt one hundred percent comfortable in a relationship. It was always one thing or another that she wanted to change about the man she was dating. When she dated Mark, he was too clingy, but David didn't call enough. John was attentive, whispering all of the right things in her ear, but not a dime or a job to his name. Not to mention his dirty fingernails. Travis was saved and treated her like a queen, but his crooked teeth and junky house drove her crazy. Ashton had too many children and seemed more interested in her brothers who played professional football than her, so that definitely wasn't going to work. Chauncey was good-looking and rich, but he put his hands on her one time too many. Will seemed perfect, but turned out to be taken.

"Elisha, are you still there?" Tonia asked, even though she could hear faint music in Elisha's background.

"I'm here."

"Girl, you know God has someone just for you."

"I know this, Tonia. I'm good."

"Are you sure? I know how you wanted things to work with Chauncey."

Elisha sucked her teeth. "Oh please, he is *old*, *old*, *old* news," she said with complete confidence. "It's been a year and I'm so glad that's over."

"Yeah, me too. I still wonder what made him up and leave town. It was like he disappeared into thin air. I mean with his mom being from the area and everything. I remember you telling me what a mama's boy he was."

"Well, all I care about is that he is gone. You were right. He was never good for me. We parted ways and I don't care to ever see him again."

"Amen to that because I know what kind of man he was. I'm just glad he never laid a hand on you again."

Elisha quietly exhaled. She had kept the beating a se-cret. The fact that Chauncey left town added that security her alarm system couldn't. Although she never told anyone about what he had done to her, Elisha was prepared in case anything had happened to her. She took pictures of her bruises and kept the medical records of the treatment she had received out of town that night safely tucked away in a folder in her closet.

"So, what do you and the hubby have planned?" Elisha cleverly shifted the conversation back on Tonia.

"Well," she said with a smile in her voice, "*if you must know*, my husband is getting off work early so that we can have dinner and a movie in."

"Oh really?"

"Yes, really." Tonia grinned. "The baby will be in the guestroom with her nana." She laughed.

"So, your mother came back?"

"No, my mother-in-law came to help out for a week. Since I go back to work on Monday, she wanted to help out my first week back."

"Aw, isn't that sweet." Elisha softened at the thought of one day having a mother-in-law as caring as Tonia's.

"It is, I know. So," she started with a sigh, "I better get off the phone and make the baby's milk and take my shower. I want to have everything squared away when she gets here in an hour. Then Rich and I can relax the entire evening and finally get a full night's sleep."

"Tonia, if I know you, sleep is the last thing on your mind," Elisha joked.

"Hey, hey, hey now," Tonia said with a chuckle. "I'm married. You just stay saved."

"Girl, you are too crazy." Elisha laughed. "Bye! I'll talk to you later."

Elisha shook her head as she moved her cell from the table to the kitchen island. Although Tonia made light of being with her husband on an intimate level, the struggle was very real for her. The celibate life Elisha lived was not an easy sell for the men she dated. It was an even tougher sale for the ones whom she actually had a relationship with. It had been difficult for her to keep a decent amount of distance from Chauncey on those out of town trips he had taken her on, but Elisha was able to not give in to temptation.

Elisha thought about when her relationship with Chauncey had changed. It was shortly after he had taken her to Costa Rica. On this trip was the third time she had to explain to him her reasons for not sleeping in the same bed with him. Although Chauncey promised that nothing would happen, deep inside Elisha felt differently. They had been in a relationship for six months at that point and upon arriving back in the States, she noticed a difference in him. It started taking him longer to call her back after she had left messages on his phone. He didn't come over when he said he would, and on certain occasions, he didn't even bother to show up.

There was a lingering suspicion that Chauncey was involved with another woman, but Elisha never accused him of cheating. She was well aware that he could most likely have any woman he wanted, and behind her back she figured that he probably did. Although she refused to sleep with him, Elisha was sure the next female would.

After setting the table with the new placemats and beautiful floral arrangement she picked up on her way home, Elisha washed the dish, butter knife, and coffee mug she had left in the sink that morning. Just as she headed to her bedroom, Tyler sent a text asking for directions. Elisha replied with her address. He sent another message that he would be there in thirty minutes. Elisha simply smiled as she grabbed her bathrobe from the doorknob and tossed her phone on the bed.

Chapter Four

"Fresh off the chopping block." Tyler held up a clear plastic bag where a slab of salmon was packed in ice. He glanced down at the other bags that sat on Elisha's doorstep before looking back to her. "I brought my mom's tabletop grill, you know, just in case." He casually winked.

"Just in case?" she questioned with a puzzled look on her face.

"Yeah, just in case." Tyler grabbed the other bags from the step with his free hand as Elisha still appeared baffled by his comment. "Oh, I guess you don't remember that incident at my place a couple years ago." He shrugged and smirked.

"Oh whatever, man." Elisha playfully snatched the bag with salmon from his hand. "I have one little mishap with an electrical appliance and you won't let me live it down." She moved to the side, allowing him room enough to enter through the front door.

Tyler chuckled as he walked into the short foyer of her home. "Well, the fire department didn't see it that way," he playfully jabbed.

"Oh, be quiet." Elisha nudged his shoulder. "I've come a *long* way since then."

"I sure hope so." Tyler raised a brow.

"Okay, you got jokes. We'll see who's laughing when I put that beat down on you." Elisha nodded repetitively with her game face on. "As I remember it, I'm still the reigning Checkers champion." She closed and locked the front door behind them. "Yeah, I don't hear you saying anything now," she egged him on.

"Well, let's just say that I've come a long way too," he confidently answered.

"Uh sure, we'll see." She gave him the sly eye as she walked past him. "Come on in, Bell, the kitchen is this way."

"Wow, I haven't heard that nickname in years," Tyler recalled. It was a name that he had gotten in high school when he used to work at a local hotel as a bellhop.

"Maybe because I'm the only one who called you that," she reminded him. "I haven't forgotten how close we were."

Tyler paused in reflection. This was one of the reasons he admired Elisha. She remembered the little things that showed she genuinely cared about him. He valued the friendship they had and even more, the person she was. Elisha was beautiful, intelligent, and witty, but she was more than that to him. She was the woman of his dreams; the confidant who was there to give him advice on what a mature woman really wanted from a man. He listened and soon fell in love with her. The moment he realized that she was the one for him, he found himself on trial for a crime he hadn't committed.

Elisha dropped the wet bag of fish in her kitchen sink and asked Tyler to place the other bags on the kitchen counter.

"You can just put your jacket on the back of a chair." She pointed towards the glass kitchen table set.

When Tyler removed his coat, his body she had only gotten a glance at earlier caused her to stare. "Hmm, someone has been putting in some work at the gym," she commented. His defined shoulders and large, sculpted arms gave his sweater great form.

Tyler held the jacket in one hand as he glanced down, following Elisha's eyes. "It must be working if you've noticed." He shamelessly flirted.

"I'm sure you get plenty of attention. I bet the girls are all over you." Elisha smirked as she dried her hands in a paper towel from the wet bag she had just handled.

"Maybe, but I'm not interested in any girls. I have my eye on a woman," he hinted, staring her down.

Elisha groaned, giving Tyler the wary eye. "Oh, please don't tell me you've hooked up with a cougar." She laughed, deflecting her prolonged gaze at his developed physique.

At first, he smiled in response, and then shook his head. "Nah, I'm rolling solo for now. But me with a cougar? I don't think so. I like 'em around my age. Pretty, smart, and independent. You know, like you," he boasted with a wink.

"Well, I'm sure you'll find her." Elisha grabbed the olive oil and seasonings for the dinner from the cupboard and placed them beside the stove.

Tyler straightened his jacket across a chair back and watched as Elisha pulled out a pot and pan from the storage door on her stove. He noticed nothing else in the room. Although dressed in an ordinary yellow fitted long-sleeved top and a pair of blue jeans, to Tyler, Elisha appeared that she had taken hours to perfect her look. She wore no makeup except for a thin layer of clear lip gloss and subtle strokes of onyx liquid eyeliner. Her hair was pulled back into a sleek ponytail, revealing a pair of studded emerald earrings.

"So, are you ready to wow me with your culinary skills?" Elisha asked as she smoothed her long ponytail to the front of one shoulder.

Tyler rubbed his hands together. "Sure, but can a brother get a hug first?"

Elisha bashfully rested a hand against her cheek before extending her arms in his direction. "I am so sorry. We haven't seen each other in years and, oh just come here." She beckoned him towards her.

"It's really good to see you again," he said into her ear. "And those earrings look nice on you."

"Thanks." She smiled, slightly leaning back with Tyler's arms still around her. "Compliments of my father on my last birthday."

They stared into one another's eyes for a beat.

"He has taste." Tyler gently touched her earlobe.

"Yeah, he does." Absorbed by his gaze, Elisha softly placed her fingers atop his hand that was near her face, but suddenly shied away from their embrace.

After suffering an uncomfortable moment of silence, Tyler asked, "Uh, can I get a tour or something? You know, this *is* my first time here." He lightly chuckled.

Shaken by her instant attraction, Elisha said, "I am so sorry. I don't know what I'm thinking." She momentarily touched her fingers to her forehead. "Sure … Come on, let me show you around."

Confused by the sudden rush of strange emotions, Elisha led Tyler on a guided tour of her house. Determined to shake what was foreign territory with him, she stopped along the way and occupied her mind by talking about the paintings and fixtures that hung on the walls. It was indeed a place she was proud to call her own.

Albeit, she had wanted to wait until she was married to purchase a home, but when it didn't happen according to her self-made timeline Elisha decided to go it alone. Especially since her two close friends who lived in town both had homes in neighboring communities. She had grown tired of apartment living and was definitely ready to move farther away from her parents. Since she wanted her own space and didn't have a husband to buy one with, she decided that this was something she'd do for herself.

"Earth to Tyler." Elisha snapped her fingers in front of his face.

"What?" He blinked from his gaze.

"I asked if you had ever been there. Cape Cod?" Elisha pointed at the picture that Charity had given her last month. It was a photograph of a rustic offshore beach house where she had edited in her designer's touch. Charity had etched in a scenic shot of sun rays bursting through clouds in the upper left corner and a breathtaking sunset in the lower right. It was a design she simply called *The Cape*.

"No, I haven't. But I wouldn't mind going there one day." He tore his eyes away from the portrait on her wall. "One for the bucket list I guess," he remarked, gazing at her.

"Bucket list or whatever you want to call it, that's where I want to go on my honeymoon." She folded her arms as they both stared back at the rolling waves in the print. "Charity hasn't stopped talking about that place ever since she and Milton came back from their *impromptu* engagement celebration."

"Oh, they went there?" Tyler asked, having already heard about the engagement from his mother.

"Yep, just a month and a half ago. They stayed at a remote little Bed and Breakfast she said Milton's friend had told him about. Isn't that sweet?" Elisha glanced at Tyler before back to the picture. "I imagine it's quaint, quiet, and so off the beaten path." She squeezed her shoulders close to her ears and then exhaled as she lowered them.

"It looks like quite the hideaway. And they went there on a whim, huh." Tyler gazed at the portrait again, as if he was trying to memorize the details.

"That's my sister. She's one of those in the moment people," Elisha hummed her words. "I guess Milton is too. After the Christmas gala, they were nowhere to be found the next morning. Come to find out, Milton had booked a flight to Boston and planned a train ride on the Cape Cod Central. Go figure, what a perfect match."

Tyler nodded, hoping that one day she'd see them in the same light. As Elisha went on about what it was like during the Christmas celebration with her brothers and sisters after Charity and Milton had returned, reminiscing about past years together, Tyler hoped that he could fit in as family too. Sure, he and Elisha had been good friends in the past, but it was just that, friends, only as close as a girl and boy could be without taking it to the next level.

As grown-ups, she had lived out of town for years and with boyfriends visiting during those special holidays, Tyler was kept at bay. It was never an issue though; he had his own life and his own girlfriends.

It didn't bother him, not until now.

Chapter Five

Tyler draped his hands in the front pockets of his jeans as the guided tour of Elisha's home drew to a close. His eyes traced along the detailed carvings of the crown molding throughout the immaculate rooms. As he followed his longtime friend back into the elaborately decorated kitchen which flowed seamlessly from the living room's elegant décor, it was obvious that her taste was impeccable.

"Let me guess, your dad's trip overseas and your mother's design ideas." Tyler's eyes roamed from the wooden cabinetry to the artful display of exotic paintings and artifacts in a lighted curio cabinet opposite a baker's rack near the patio door. "Am I right?" His expression read that he already knew the answer.

"Oh, how well do you know me, let me count the ways," Elisha teased. "You're right. Mama designed the kitchen. And well, the rest of the house too," she admitted with a chuckle. "And Daddy, well, he hasn't changed. Singing all over the world and still bringing his girls something special back from his trips."

"Your father is a good man." A bit of preoccupation shadowed his countenance as he pulled grocery from the bags he had brought in earlier. "The kind of father I always wanted in my life. After my dad left Mama, Mr. Maxwell was somebody I really looked up to. But with the way things went down with the case and your mother being DA and all, things just got kind of awkward."

"I see your point. If it's any consolation, he used to ask about you." Elisha's face held a reflective gaze. "After the trial, he would mention you every now and then, but after we lost touch—"

"We didn't lose touch, Elisha. You just started ignoring my calls."

"Okay Tyler, let's not go down memory lane again. At least not that road." She forcefully tore a couple pieces of aluminum foil and placed them aside on the counter. "You're here now. Back then I wanted to keep the peace in my family. I had my mother on one side and you on the other. What was I supposed to do?"

"Trust your friend." His voice inched up a notch. "Somebody you've known since you were a kid."

"But she's my mother." Elisha gripped the plastic bag of salmon that was in the sink and stared at Tyler. "I wanted to stick up for you, but I honestly didn't know where you were that night. I couldn't lie."

Still frustrated and somewhat angered by the past, Tyler's volume edged even higher. "And being the good lawyer she is you just couldn't convince her that I wasn't that type of man."

"First of all, you need to lower your voice." Elisha widened her eyes as she pointed at him.

Tyler looked away, exhaled, and then turned back toward her. "Look, I'm sorry." His apology carried sincerity. "I-I shouldn't be taking this all out on you."

"No, you shouldn't." Elisha slowly shook her head and resumed removing the slab of fish from the bag. "Besides, you were acquitted. I mean, aren't things going well for you now?"

Tyler meticulously rubbed his hands together. Although he didn't appreciate the way Elisha diminished the ordeal he had experienced, she was right, he was doing well for himself. In fact, better than expected. With eight years on the police force in Lewiston Springs, aside from the assault accusation, his reputation was impeccable. He had a glowing recommendation from the Chief of Police when he transferred and soon made detective of the year at his new duty station in Memphis. Things in his life were good, but as he gazed at Elisha he knew they could be so much better.

"You're right. I guess it's just a sore spot with me because whenever I come home to visit, people are always looking at me funny. I hate being labeled something that I'm not."

"Welcome to the real world." Elisha instinctively raised an eyebrow. "And weren't you always the one telling me to forget about what people thought as long as I'm pleasing God?"

Tyler nodded as that was a key phrase he used to constantly repeat to her whenever she would vent about the things going on in her life. Whether it was when long-standing teachers grumbled at the fact that she was too young to be assistant principal at the elementary school where she now worked or the day she was unexpectedly promoted to interim principal, and then a month later to principal. Tyler used to be the one always telling Elisha to focus on the Lord and not people. It was easy for him to say that until he faced his own trials.

"And for the record, I'm sorry for not calling you back then," she apologized. "I guess I was angry that you were even involved in such a mess. We were close and it made me angry to learn that a woman was raped and you were even implicated."

"Did it ever dawn on you that I was working a case? The woman's brother was a dealer." Tyler placed his hands on the counter and leaned towards her. "I know we were close, but at the time I couldn't tell you about the investigation. I was just doing my job as a cop. Now, I'm sorry that lady was assaulted, but you had to know that I wasn't like that."

"I didn't know what to think. There was evidence and—"

"There was no evidence," he insisted, cutting her off, "at least not on me. Since they didn't know who committed the crime, she and her brother tried to pin it on me."

With a confused look on her face, Elisha questioned, "But why you? You weren't the only officer investigating the case. I was just trying to figure out why they would target only you."

Tyler sighed in response. He paced to the other side of the room and parked a hand at his waist while dragging the other one down across his mouth.

Elisha stared at him as he faced the patio the door. "What is it?"

"I never thought she would take it that way."

"What are you talking about?" Elisha grimaced.

Tyler turned around to face her with regret in his eyes. "I used that woman to get information on her brother."

"*What*? What do you mean you *used* her?"

"It's not what you think." Tyler raised his hands in defense before her mind began formulating all sorts of unwarranted accounts.

"Well, please tell me what you're talking about." Her eyebrows furrowed as she waited for an explanation.

"She sort of came on to me when I was on a break. You know that little café downtown, *Melisa's*?"

"Yeah, I know it." She nodded, dividing her attention between him and the fish she had just rinsed and arranged on the piece of foil positioned on her counter.

"That's where she used to work. My partner and I were having a bite to eat. We were both dressed in casual clothes at the time about to head out to a football game. Anyway, when she took our orders she flirted a little, passed me her number and told me to call her. She was new in town and wanted me to show her around. I had no interest in her at all, believe me, but my partner mentioned that we could use that to our advantage. Besides, I was just finishing up my bachelor's degree and building my experience as a detective. We needed to take this guy down and she was a direct link to him. I had to take a chance."

"And she turned on you."

"This city ain't exactly a large metropolis, so word eventually got back to her. Long story short, she was assaulted, didn't see who did it and made me the fall guy. The rest is history."

"Why didn't you tell me this before?" Elisha questioned.

"I tried, but you weren't trying to hear me. Besides, your mother made a convincing argument. I know, I know … that's her job."

"It *was* her job."

The expression on Tyler's face sought clarification.

"She retired from the county a couple months ago. Didn't your mother tell you?"

"Oh yeah-yeah, I heard. But isn't she still licensed and accepting clients?"

Elisha cracked a smile. "Hmm, you know more about my family than you lead on."

Tyler bashfully grinned. "Not too much, just enough, you know."

"Uh huh, I know." Elisha nodded, still unconvinced.

"So, I guess things were a little uncomfortable with my mother and you at work during the time of the trial."

"No, your mother is a great teacher and things were pretty much normal. Why? Did she say that?" Elisha wondered as she stared Tyler squarely in the eyes.

"No, she didn't." He shook his head. "She never grouped you and your mother into one category."

"Oh, you mean like you did?"

"Now Elisha, that's not what I did." He shot her a daring look. "I'm just saying that ... oh, never mind."

They both stared at one another before bursting into laughter.

"You know we could go back and forth like this all night, right? Let's just put that behind us. Today is a new day and why don't we start with a clean slate, okay?"

"Okay," she responded with a nod.

"So, it's all good now." Tyler moved alongside Elisha and rolled up his sleeves. "But I just want you to do one thing for me."

"What's that?" Elisha asked as she poured rice from a bag into a bowl.

He took the bowl from her hands and pointed across the room. "Take a seat. Tonight, this is my territory."

She held her hands up and said, "Yes, officer. Anything you say."

Tyler chuckled as Elisha backed towards her kitchen table as if she were under arrest.

"And can I get a little mood music while I work?" He cooked best when moving melodies filled the airwaves around him.

"Sure, what did you want to hear?"
"Something soulful and uplifting," Tyler suggested. "Maybe that CD your dad released last spring."

"Oh yeah, I'm always jamming to Daddy's songs. Give me a second." Elisha activated her wireless sound system to play her father's CD in the kitchen. "I really like track three on that album. And I am so feeling that duet on track five." She made mention of the Gospel artist her father, Gerald, had collaborated with. "I've been meaning to buy her album for months now, but I just haven't."

"I'm going to have to check that out myself."
Just then Elisha's cell began ringing from the living room. "Hey, hang on. Let me see who's calling me."

Elisha rushed from the kitchen to the next room and grabbed her phone from the living room table where she had left it when Tyler arrived. When she looked at the lighted screen, her lips instinctively parted. His number was the last one she expected to see scrolling across her phone.

Chapter Six

Elisha silenced the volume on her cell as she stared aimlessly at the incoming call. Of all the people to dial her number on this day, he was next to the last person she expected to call. The phone rang once more before she hesitantly answered.

"Hello?" Her voice mirrored the confusion she felt.

"Hey," the familiar stranger replied. His voice low and terse, just as it was the last time they had spoken. "How are you?"

"Uh, I'm fine." She swallowed the uncomfortable lump in her throat.

"Do you have a minute to talk?" he asked as if they were old friends who had just spoken yesterday.

Elisha's forehead wrinkled in confusion. "Why?"

"I just—"

"Hang on for a sec." Elisha rolled her eyes as she took the phone from her ear. She pressed the mute button and sighed. *Why is Will calling me now?* With mixed emotions Elisha slowly walked back into the kitchen where Tyler was and told him, "I have to take this call, but I'll only be a minute."

"Sure." Tyler tore his attention away from the seasonings and vegetables on the countertop. "Is everything okay?"

"Oh yeah, everything is fine," she assured him. "Just continue doing what you're doing. I'll be back in a minute." She started to walk away, but then stopped short and turned around to face him. "There's juice and lemonade in the fridge. The glasses are—"

"I think I can find a cup somewhere in here." Tyler winked with a slight smirk. "This kitchen can't be too different from all the others I've seen in my life."

Elisha smiled at his comment, and then started for her bedroom. Once behind the closed door, she briefly stared at the phone before she released the mute. "Are you still there?"

"I'm here … *so*, how's everything going?"

"Oh me, I'm fine," Elisha sarcastically answered as she walked towards her window. "*So*, how are you and your *fiancée?*"

"I'm not engaged," he flatly replied.

"What?" Elisha grimaced and dropped a hand to her hip. "But you told me that you were getting married. Remember that?"

"I know what I told you then …" Will took a breath and started again. "I don't want to do this over the phone. Can I come over?"

"You're in town?" She instinctively peered through her blinds.

"Yeah, I'm in town. Just for a few hours though. A development meeting for work. So, can I see you? I'll explain everything then."

Elisha looked away from Tyler's car that was parked in her driveway and questioned, "What is there to explain?"

"A lot. You have every right to be angry with me, but please let me explain."

Against her better judgment, Elisha allowed her hard-core wall to collapse. "What time were you talking?"

"In an hour."

Elisha scrunched her lips, wondering why he still had such a hold over her.

"Is that all right?" He sought confirmation.

"*One hour,*" Elisha emphasized. "Not a minute later."

With a chuckle in his voice, he answered, "I promise."

"Okay, I'll be here." She sighed, and then confirmed her address with him, although he knew it already.

Once she ended the call, Elisha composed herself and calmly walked back into the kitchen. There she saw Tyler searing the salmon to perfection. On the counter she saw a pile of diced onions and red bell peppers on the cutting board. Tyler looked like he was in his own world moving around the kitchen like he belonged there.

"Hey," Elisha droned.

"Hey." Tyler glanced at her before looking back down to the glass pan greased with olive oil. "Do you have any sea salt? I promise I won't use much, just a dash to give it some more *flava*," he teased, altering the word flavor with a southern drawl.

"Um yeah," she said, gently scratching her temple, and then pointed. "In the cabinet over the stove."

"Oh good." Tyler grabbed the sea salt and sat it next to the other seasonings on the counter. "I hope you don't mind, but I decided to sear the salmon instead and let it bake in the oven the rest of the time. It'll give the marinade more time to soak in."

"No, that's fine, but uh, I hate to do this. Something just came up."

"Oh, you mean with your phone call?" He effectively divided his attention between her and the fish sizzling on the stove.

"Yeah, the phone call." She fidgeted with her long ponytail. "Do you think that maybe we can have a rain check on dinner?"

"A rain check?" Tyler sounded crushed, but successful in his attempt to conceal it. "Oh, you need me to leave?"

"I'm sorry, but there's something I really need to take care of."

"Oh, okay. Sure." He glanced back at the fish on the stove before looking back to her. "Well, they're pretty much crusted. Do you still want me to put them in the oven or—"

"Oh no, don't worry about that." She waved her hand in his direction. "I can just throw them in the oven. Maybe we can have them for lunch or something tomorrow."

"Right." Tyler studied her movements as she temporarily avoided eye contact. He knew her well enough to know that this was about another man. "We can do that." He nodded and turned the stove off. After he wiped his hands in the folded apron around his waist, Tyler pulled it off and tossed it aside.

"It's just a last minute thing." Elisha struggled to gain eye contact with him as he walked past her. "You understand, right?"

"Yeah, of course," Tyler said, clearing his face of disappointment. "Hey, you have something to handle, go ahead and handle it. I promised Nathan that we'd get up when I got in town anyway." He made mention of his former partner on the police force. "I'll see what he's up to."

Elisha watched as Tyler gathered up a bag of trash from beneath her kitchen sink. "Oh, you don't have to do that."

"Hey, when I make a mess, I clean it up," he matter-of-factly said. "Besides, you don't want old fish bags stinking up the place." He offered a soft smile. "So, is the big can out back?"

Elisha softened at his kind gesture and nodded. "Yes, right through the patio door."

Tyler opened the sliding door that led to a spacious deck and dumped the trash outside. Once back inside he said, "You should really keep this door locked. Just because you have a gate, anybody could still get in."

"Yes, father," Elisha joked. "You really take your job with you everywhere."

"Better to be safe than sorry." He locked the patio door behind him.

Elisha gazed as he washed his hands, and then pulled his coat from the chair he had hung it on earlier. Tyler then motioned for her to escort him to the front door. Elisha's eyes drifted away from his as she walked ahead of him to the front door.

She waved as Tyler got into his vehicle. He raised a hand and backed out of her driveway.

After closing the front door, Elisha considered how ridiculous Tonia would say she was being for even entertaining the idea of dating Will again, but she didn't care. Although he caused her to cry for almost a week straight last month, she was incredibly tired of being single. If there was a chance that things may still work with the man she thought would have been her perfect match, she was ready to explore that possibility.

Chapter Seven

Elisha rushed to her bedroom closet and pushed several hangers aside to get her favorite burgundy sweater. She was saving the new classic knit cardigan to wear to church on Sunday, but this evening seemed as good a time as any for her to model the top. The sleek fabric with the wrap-around belt was just what she needed Will to see draped across her trim body. Elisha glanced in the door-length mirror, noting that the fitted jeans she wore paired with it perfectly. She quickly exchanged her studded earrings for the silver, shimmering hoop ones instead. After adding a layer of rose tinted gloss to her lips, Elisha's modified look was almost complete.

She hurriedly pulled her hair loose from the ponytail holder and ran her fingers through the strands that fell past her shoulders. After making a part on one side in the front of her silky mane, Elisha smiled to herself. Will adored her hair in this style. She grabbed the heart-shaped glass vial of perfume from her shelf that he had mailed to her at Christmas, and sprayed it on the sides of her neck.

Elisha lingered with the bottle in her hand, somewhat realizing her desperation. Her shoulders slumped as she considered all the lies ex-boyfriends had told her in past relationships, and then she thought about Will. He hadn't actually lied to her. She admitted to herself that she wanted a relationship so badly that she somehow concocted one in her head with this man. He never asked her to be his exclusive girlfriend. He never introduced her to family or friends. And he never asked to meet anyone in her family.

Maybe he was simply being a nice friend to me, she reasoned. That was the only logical explanation she had. After all, Elisha had never expressed an interest to be more than that either. *But he had to know that I was interested in him*, she supposed. They had spent hours on the phone and texted one another every day. She appeared giddy just at the sound of his voice. *Was he that naïve? Or maybe I just read too much into it*, she justified. There was no way for him to know what was in her mind, but then why would he call and ask to explain? This was something Elisha desperately wanted, no, *needed* to know. Either way, no matter what the reasoning behind his sudden disappearance, she wanted to look good when he saw her.

Elisha glanced at the wall clock in her bedroom and quickly kicked off her homely flip-flops and slid into a pair of designer ankle-length leather boots.

Since she didn't have time to freshen the house to her satisfaction, Elisha continued cooking the meal Tyler had started. When the timer on the stove buzzed she dashed into the kitchen and removed the salmon from the oven.

She glanced at the time on the microwave. One hour and twenty-five minutes had passed since Will had called.

Elisha looked out of her front window and there was no sign of life. The driveway was as vacant as her eyes that stared aimlessly down the street. She walked back into the kitchen and picked up her cell. Elisha reluctantly sent a text message to Will asking of his whereabouts. *Maybe traffic was bad*, she presumed. There was no response to her text.

She typed another message, but quickly deleted it. Just as she was about to put the phone down, it started to ring. There was no numerical display on her screen.

"Hello?" Elisha answered.

There was no answer.

"Hello?" she repeated.

Still, no one responded.

Elisha took the phone from her ear and stared at the screen. Suddenly, the call ended.

Several minutes later, there was another incoming call. With hesitation she picked up.

"Hey, I think I'm outside of your house." Will sounded unsure.

Elisha got up from her kitchen table, momentarily discarding all of the bad thoughts she was having about him and walked to the front door. When she looked outside there was a black Camry in her driveway. She lowered the phone from her ear as he turned the head-lights off and opened the car door.

"I know I'm late." Will glanced at his wrist watch as he strolled up her walkway. "But I took a wrong turn and got lost. I tried to call, but the reception was bad. The community across the highway is like a jungle with all of those trees." He extended his hands once he was within arm's length and hugged her. "Anyway, it's good to see you." Will took a step back and examined her from head to toe. "Wow, you look great."

"Thanks, you too." Elisha blushed. "And I'm glad you found the place. I guess I'll let you off the hook since you haven't been here in a while." Elisha wanted to be angry with him, but she couldn't. After he flashed his gorgeous smile, her heart helplessly melted. "Come on in."

Will closed the front door behind him and followed Elisha to the living room sofa. There he rested a hand on her knee. After a moment of pleasantries and more compliments from Will, Elisha could feel in her soul that he was about to share something that she probably didn't want to hear. Her eyes traveled from his hand perched on her knee to the other one on his chin.

Will looked off in another direction as he said, "I have something to tell you."

"What is it?" Elisha scooted to the edge of the sofa where he was and angled her head in a way that pulled his face back towards hers.

"Well, for starters, I apologize for the way I just dropped things between us."

His confession served as some sort of consolation for her that she wasn't delusional. There had indeed been something more to their friendship.

"I never wanted to hurt you. I was falling for you ... *hard*." He nervously chuckled.

Elisha gently nodded, having believed that she had felt the same way.

"But the thought of having my child so—"

"*Child*?" The mood abruptly changed as her eyes narrowed to slits.

Will casually nodded in response.

"You never mentioned having a child." Elisha gently pushed his hand from her knee. "How old is this child?"

"Her name is Sophia." Will slowly folded his hand into the other. "And she's four."

Elisha blankly stared at him, and then quickly looked away. "What else aren't you telling me, Will?" She stood and walked a few steps towards the fireplace before she faced him again.

"Please don't be upset. It's just that after New Year's Day, my ex up and told me that she was moving to Arizona where her sister lived." Will shook his head as if he was reliving that moment all over again. "I couldn't let her take my child over twenty hours away."

"So you asked her to marry you instead?"

"I know it sounds crazy, but I didn't know what else to do. I-I wasn't thinking. Now that I've had some time to figure things out, I know that I couldn't marry somebody like her."

"But you can have a baby with her?" The mere thought that he had a child with another woman burned her with anger.

"Elisha, that was over four years ago. We did the on and off again thing, but she's nothing like you." He walked over to where she now stood and rested his hands on her shoulders. "You are the kind of woman a man dreams about. I certainly didn't want to lead you on. That's why I kept my distance. I wasn't sure where things stood with me and Monica. You know how it can be when you have a child with someone."

"No, I don't know." Elisha raised a brow and moved away from him. "I don't have any children." She plopped down on the sofa again.

"I didn't mean it like that." Will exhaled a long sigh. "Elisha, I want *you*. I have ever since I met you last fall … I just didn't know if things were really over between me and my daughter's mother. Now, I know," he said confidently.

"So, things are really over?" She buried her eyes into his. "I mean *really* over."

"*Yes.*" He sat down beside her. "I wanted to get that chapter in my life settled before asking you to be my girl, my woman." He scooted closer to her. "That's if you'll have me."

This was not the way Elisha envisioned the beginning of a relationship with Will. His sweet notes and endearing texts had made her feel like a princess, but now their attraction seemed somewhat marred. It wasn't only the fact that he had a child, but also because he never told her about someone whom he said was so important in his life. She knew the deal about baby mama drama from a guy she had dated in college, but hoped this Monica person was different.

"Will you have me?"

Elisha contemplated Will's question. If he had asked her that a month ago, she would have answered before he had finished asking. But now, she pondered it a little more carefully. Her list had four simple things she wanted from a man in this order: *Loves God, financially independent, no children, and spontaneously romantic.*

She mentally crossed number three off her list and noted that number two was in jeopardy. The fact that he had a child testified to that. It would only take a few unexpected bills or an increase in child support payments to blow that one completely off the list. Nonetheless,

Elisha figured that he loved God since they've had several deep conversations about Him. And after she gazed up at the bouquet of red roses he had retrieved from his vehicle along with a fuzzy stuffed animal, Elisha was delighted. Despite his efforts, she felt that he needed improvement with number four on her list as well.

"So, are we together?" Will repeated his previous sentiment, this time gazing at her the way he had when they first met.

Elisha softly smiled as she fought off the nagging notion that she shouldn't compromise. But instead of listening to what her heart truly felt, she told Will, "Yes."

Chapter Eight

"So man, tell me what's up?" Nathan asked after he scored his third straight basket on Tyler. "You're off your game today," he joked, enjoying a friendly basketball game of twenty-one at the neighborhood rec center. "If you keep this up, I may as well play by myself."

Distracted, Tyler panted, "Uh huh," as his tank top hung like a wet rag from his body.

"All right, all right." Nathan stopped his hustle and palmed the ball. "What's up?" He briefly glanced to the other side of the court where four teenagers were paired up in two teams, playing a similar game.

"I saw Elisha last night."

"Oh yeah?" Nathan looked back at Tyler. "What's going on with her?"

"She still got it, man." Tyler angled his head with a look that said more than his words.

"I haven't seen her in a minute, but I bet she does." Nathan grinned as he wiped the dripping sweat from his forehead with the back of his hand.

"Hey, are you guys finished over here?" a teenager asked as he stood mid-court, looking back and forth between Tyler and Nathan.

"Yeah man, it's all yours." Nathan tossed the ball to the teenager, and then motioned for Tyler to join him on the sideline.

They both grabbed towels from their bags and sat on the bleachers. Nathan passed a bottle of water to Tyler before he took a swig from his own.

"So, what's the problem?"

"Problem?" Tyler looked confused.

"Uh, you were talking about Elisha," Nathan reminded him.

"Oh yeah." Tyler shook his head and looked his long-time friend in the eyes. "Well, since I left, man, I've been thinking about her."

"Thinking about her?"

"Yeah, you know, *thinking* about her." The widening of Tyler's eyes emphasized his point.

"Oh, oh, I get it." Nathan pointed with a sly grin. "So have you told her?"

"No," Tyler answered with a sigh. "I think she's seeing some other guy."

"So what, you afraid of a little competition?" Nathan laughed and took another gulp of water from his bottle.

"Afraid, man please." Tyler blew him off. "My game is tight."

"All right, all right. If it's so tight, what's the problem then?"

"Haven't you been listening to anything I've been saying? I just told you that she may be seeing some other cat."

"Man, listen to yourself. *Seeing some other cat?*" Nathan mocked. "Straight up, if you want this girl, you better go get her. How do you think I got Janet?"

"Yeah, but that's different."

"How so?"

"Y'all haven't been friends since you were kids. She already knew what was up when you approached her."

"True, true …"

"Things are little different with me and Elisha. She's always been a friend. There's never been anything else between us. See, you and Janet knew what was up from the moment you stepped to her."

"I see your point, man."

"Anyway, what's going on with her? How is Janet?"

"Oh she's good. She's *real* good." Nathan then proudly announced, "I proposed last night after dinner. You know, the whole Valentine's romance thing. Women eat that kind of stuff up."

"You 'ole sly dog you." Tyler hit Nathan on the shoulder with his fist and nodded knowingly. "So that's why you didn't answer your phone when I called."

"Yep. I had to show her that last night was about her."

"She's really the one, huh?"

"She better be. That ring set me back a few grand." Nathan released a throaty laugh. "She's the one alright. After a year of dating, she had dropped enough hints that even a blind man could see."

"Oh, it was like that?" Tyler grinned as he pulled a sweatshirt from his bag and pulled it over his head.

"Yeah. One time when I went to her place there was no less than three magazines turned to the pages of ring ads. One in the kitchen, one on the coffee table, and one on the foyer table right when you walk through the door. She probably had one in the bathroom too." Nathan chuckled. "But seriously, I wanted to make her my wife anyway. She's one of those women that you don't meet every day. Know what I mean?" He took another gulp and emptied the water bottle. "Janet is real. She got the looks, the smarts, *and* the God. No matter what, you need a praying woman in your corner." He pointed at Tyler.

Tyler nodded in response. He agreed with everything Nathan had just said and knew Elisha embodied all of those qualities and more.

"So, when are you going to tell her?"

Tyler carelessly shrugged. "I don't know if I should."

"What? Wait a minute, you just told me that you want this woman and now you don't know if you should tell her?"

"Man, you know how close Elisha and I have been. We go way back. What if she sees me as a brother or something?"

"Look, you're *not* her brother. Yeah, you may have been close or whatever, but it's been like two years since y'all last saw each other. I'm sure that brotherly love, if that's what she saw, has worn off by now," he kidded, and then hit Tyler on the chest with the back of his hand. "Or look at it this way, maybe she's feeling the same thing about you. You ever thought about that?"

Tyler took Nathan's words to heart. It was possible that Elisha saw him the same way he saw her, but it just unnerved him to make his feelings known. There was the lingering issue with her mother and how she grilled him on the witness stand. Tyler wondered if Elisha would hold back because of that since she clearly made it known that she wanted to keep the peace in her family.

"What if you're wrong?" Tyler questioned, having backpedaled on sharing his feelings with Elisha for a while now.

"Bottom line, this is not about me. I'm just letting you know what *I* would do in your situation. I mean, what do you have to lose? Y'all weren't on speaking terms anyway, right?"

"Gee thanks, that's not what I wanted to hear."

"Hey man, I'm just trying to get you to see the big picture. Think about it. You know this woman. You know she's honest, would never play you, *and* you got history." Nathan counted Elisha's traits out on his fingers. "Again, I ask, what do you have to lose?"

Tyler pondered his friend's advice. He had always been straight with him, on and off the job when they used to work together. Tyler figured that if he let these two weeks go by without sharing his feelings with Elisha, the next time she may be married to someone else. And that was not a chance he was willing to take.

Chapter Nine

Elisha sat on the edge of her bed, noting that there was something different in Tyler's voice. They had made plans to cash their rain check today and he was due to arrive at her house in less than twenty minutes. Aside from the fact that she and Will ate the dinner he had bought and started cooking last night, Elisha felt horrible that there was nothing in her kitchen prepared to eat.

When Will left her house last night, Elisha laid awake in bed for hours. She had watched a movie on TV, but still couldn't rest. After she said her evening prayer, Elisha was finally able to drift off to sleep. And when she did, she had an interesting dream.

Elisha rested on her bed and replayed the dream in her mind for the third time today. It was a fresh, spring day and there was love in the air. The birds were chirping, the bees buzzing from one flower to another, and decora-tions elegantly garnished the white wooden staircase leading up the steps of her local church. Somebody was getting married.

A black, stretched Escalade pulled into the parking lot of the church. When the driver opened the back door, the woman who emerged from the seat was her. Elisha saw herself outfitted in a stunning ivory shade gown, smiling endlessly. In a blink of the eye, she was at the altar, staring at her husband-to-be. To her dismay, she couldn't see past his mouth as that was the focal point in her vision. She read his lips that mouthed the words *I do*, and then she gazed at her hands as a sparkling band was placed on her finger to match the engagement ring already there.

He knew her taste well and, in the dream, she was genuinely happy.

Ding-dong!

Jolted from her daze Elisha's eyes fluttered as the doorbell rang for the second time. She peered out her window and saw Tyler's vehicle parked in the driveway. She looked at the digital clock on her nightstand which read three twenty-six. He arrived promptly as promised with four minutes to spare.

"I'm coming!" Elisha yelled, sure that Tyler couldn't hear her, but she made the effort anyway. She glanced at her reflection in the dresser mirror and gently smoothed a few strands of hair that were out of place on her way to the front door.

"Right on time," Elisha said before her eyes drifted to Tyler's hands. "What's this?"

"Lunch." Tyler glanced at the box of pizza in his hand and the bottle of diet soda sitting on the step, and then looked back to her. "I figured since I didn't finish the rice last night that maybe you'd be in the mood for something else. Besides, I sort of had a craving." He winked. "But I can still finish the rice if you want me to."

Elisha shifted her eyes away from him and shook her head, embarrassed that she finished cooking the rice and then ate it with another man. "No, pizza sounds good right about now."

"Oh, and before I forget, I got that CD you were talking about yesterday." Tyler reached inside of his coat with his free hand and pulled out the case. "I checked out the songs and they're nice."

"Oh, you didn't have to do that." She looked at this man who had paid attention to the details of her desires. At any other time in her life, this would have seemed minor, but today his sincerity struck her off guard. "Thank you, Tyler …"

"Anytime," he replied with warmth in his words. "So, uh, can I come in?" He stared at the way she barricaded the doorway.

They both smiled at one another as she moved aside and motioned for him to enter.

Elisha quickly sat the CD down on the foyer table and reached for the pizza box. "Here, I'll take that. I don't know how you knew I was hungry, but we can eat now." She rubbed her stomach, leading the way into the kitchen.

Tyler watched Elisha's movements as she reached into the cupboard and retrieved two plates from the middle shelf. She then took two decorative glasses from the dishwasher and placed them on the counter.

"Ice?" she asked him, holding one of the glasses up in her hand.

"Yeah," Tyler answered, almost mesmerized by the simplest outfits Elisha wore.

The plain white t-shirt with gold metallic letters simply spelled out, *Jesus Saves*, in bold cursive print. Bearing that name alone made her more attractive than any woman he had ever dated. Her glowing skin was still a beautiful canvas even without makeup. Her long hair was in an up do secured by a basic black clip that revealed her plunging neckline. Tyler also noticed the chain around Elisha's neck adorned with a jeweled purple ribbon.

"Here you are." Elisha sat a plate and a glass filled with ice on the kitchen table in front of him.

"Thank you," he said, and then cleared his throat. "So which one?" Tyler questioned as his eyes drifted from hers back to the chain dangling from her neck.

"What do you mean?" Her eyes followed his as she sat her glass on the table too.

"The necklace … the purple ribbon. Which cause does it represent?" He pulled the bottle of soda towards him and began filling both glasses. "You know, some people wear it in remembrance of the victims of 9-11, some for child abuse, others for certain cancers, and well, the list goes on," he clarified. "Which cause are you supporting?"

"Oh … uh," Elisha nervously began, and then clutched the small ribbon in the palm of her hand. "I'm against domestic violence."

"Oh yeah? Why domestic violence?"

"What? Do you advocate a man beating on a woman?" she snapped, her eyes piercing into his.

"No, of course not," Tyler defended himself. "But some women beat on men who refuse to hit them back too you know," he rebutted.

"So, whose side are you on?" Elisha raised her voice.

Soon there was a stark break of silence.

Tyler dared not intrude any further as Elisha seemed uneasy even being questioned about the small piece of jewelry. She reached across the table for the devotional notebook she had left there earlier and accidentally knocked over one of the glasses filled with soda. Her hands nervously shook as she tried to clean it up.

Tyler grabbed a dish towel from the counter a few feet away and rushed to her side. "Here, let me help you."

"I can take care of myself!" Elisha snatched the towel from him.

Tyler froze, staring at her like someone he didn't know.

Elisha paused, momentarily closing her eyes, and then apologized. "I'm sorry. I-I didn't mean to yell at you."

"It's okay."

"No, it's not." Elisha shook her head. "Please, just excuse me for a minute." She dropped the towel on the table and pushed past him.

Tyler followed her to her bedroom and knocked on the closed door. "Elisha, are you okay?"

"Yes," she said in between sniffles.

"Are you sure?"

"I'm okay. I'll be out in a minute."

"All right," Tyler reluctantly answered, but lingered outside the door.

Elisha stood in front of the mirror in her bathroom and patted her dampened cheeks. "You've got to get over this," she whispered to herself. The fact that Chauncey was still somewhere out on the streets troubled her. Although she still had the photos and medical records from the time he had beaten her last year tucked away in her closet, Elisha was resolved to move on. *It has been a whole year. Don't let him take your sanity.* She exhaled a breath before walking out of her bathroom and opening her bedroom door.

"Are you sure you're all right?" Tyler met eyes with Elisha. "You know I'm here for you."

"I know." Elisha nodded and hugged her old friend. "And I'm fine … *really*," she tried to convince him.

"Do you want to talk about it?"

Tyler had been a sounding board for Elisha in the past, but today she wasn't quite ready for him to see her in this new light. She felt that if anybody should know about what had happened to her last year, it should be her new boyfriend.

"You know we always talked about everything." His words were sincere.

"I know," she said through her stuffy nose, "but I'd rather not."

"Okay, no pressure." Tyler gently touched her shoulder.

Elisha cleared her throat and moved away from him. "So, are you ready for your Checkers beat-down?" She tried to act as if nothing had ever happened.

Tyler hesitantly chuckled. "Right after I throw down with that pizza in the kitchen."

Mindful that she had just shown her vulnerability to this man, Elisha tried desperately to recapture her strength. He had always seen her strong, vibrant, and in control of her feelings. This was the way she preferred that it remained. Outside of when family members passed, Elisha had never allowed Tyler to see her shed a tear, until now.

After an interactive lunch catching up on old times, the two settled into the living room for several rounds of a spirited board game. Tyler and Elisha sat on the floor opposite each other with their backs against the couch and loveseat respectively. The game was on the coffee table that sat in between them. As promised, Elisha beat him three times in a row. She seemed to be completely back to her old self as she gloated about winning the games.

Tyler joked about how he let her win, but he was preoccupied. He fidgeted with his coat when she left the room to refresh their drinks and pulled something from his pocket. When Elisha reentered the room, he asked her to sit next to him on the sofa as they prepared to watch the movie he had rented.

Almost an hour into the flick, Tyler draped his arm across Elisha's shoulder. She looked at his arm and then into his eyes. She saw something she hadn't seen before and then caved in when Tyler passionately planted his lips onto hers. Several seconds had passed before Elisha placed a hand on his chest and gently pushed him back.

"We can't do this," she softly said, backing away from him.

Tyler searched her eyes for truth because the way she started to kiss him back had said otherwise.

"We're just friends." Her words contradicted her emotions as she staved off the desire to kiss him again.

"Yeah, right, we're just friends." Tyler cleared the perimeter of his lips of moisture with his fingertips. "I'm sorry about that."

"No, no, you don't have to apologize. You just sort of got caught up in the moment." Elisha cleverly placed the entire attraction on him. "We were just hanging, right?"

"Oh yeah … yeah, we were just hanging." He uneasily nodded.

"Besides …" Elisha shifted her eyes away from him. "I have a boyfriend."

"*You have a boyfriend?*" He raised an eyebrow. "I thought you were single."

"I was," Elisha candidly responded. "It sort of just happened."

Tyler grunted to himself and guessed, "The call last night. Did an old boyfriend come over?"

"Something like that."

"Isn't that something." Tyler patted down his pant pockets and quickly pulled his keys out. "I guess I better go."

"Already?" Elisha watched as he stood. "The movie still has about thirty minutes left." She pointed at the television, and then looked to him for a different answer.

"Yeah, I better. I don't think your boyfriend would appreciate my kissing you," Tyler said with a hint of sarcasm. He grabbed his coat that was on the seat next to her. "Besides, I've seen this movie before anyway."

"Why would you rent a movie that you've seen before?"

"Because you said that you hadn't seen it." His prolonged gaze said more than his words.

"Oh …" Elisha slid her feet into a pair of slippers, and then stood. "So, did you want to come over tomorrow?"

Tyler touched his temple as if in deep thought. "No, tomorrow isn't good. I promised my mother that I'd take her out before she goes in Monday for the surgery."

"Oh yeah, that's right. Her surgery is next week." Elisha quietly cleared her throat and nodded. "But you're going to church though, right?"

"Of course. You know it," Tyler answered, somewhat distracted. "We're visiting my aunt's church." He fidgeted with the keys in his hands. "Okay then, I'm gonna get out of here."

Elisha followed him into the foyer. After he put his coat on, she hugged him in the open doorway.

"Drive safely," she whispered into his ear.

Unable to resist the urge to hold her, Tyler wrapped his arms around her waist and gently squeezed her closer. "It was good seeing you, Elisha," he whispered back in her ear, and then pecked her on the cheek. "I'll catch up with you next week sometime."

Next week? Elisha slowly released his embrace and stared as Tyler quickly walked to his vehicle. She folded her arms from the cold weather and raised a hand as he turned on his headlights. After he backed out of the driveway, she closed her door and activated the alarm.

Elisha placed the pillows on her leather sofa back into a neat arrangement and inadvertently ran across a small, red rectangular shaped envelope on the floor barely visible from underneath her couch. *What's this?* Elisha's eyes narrowed as she rotated the envelope from front to back and found both sides blank. When she opened it and found a heart wrenching note from Tyler about how he truly wanted their friendship to grow into a relationship, her jaw unconsciously dropped.

Elisha grabbed her cell phone and started a text to Tyler, but quickly deleted the message. She held the phone in her hand, glaring at the illuminated screen for several seconds before it went dark. He was sweet and definitely attentive, but she had made a commitment to Will.

After that kiss with Tyler though, Elisha questioned if it was a commitment that she was truly willing to keep.

Chapter Ten

"I was wondering when you were going to come back over to see your Godchild," Tonia squawked with a hand on her hip after she opened her front door. "I figured my child would be walking by the time you saw her again," she joked.

Elisha playfully rolled her eyes and giggled. "Girl, move out of my way and let me in." She laughed as she pushed past Tonia and strutted inside of the house.

It had been two days since she last spoke to Tonia and a week since she last saw her in person. After Elisha shared with her a couple days ago the feelings Tyler said he had, Tonia confessed that she saw it coming. Taken aback, Elisha pondered if there was ever an unspoken attraction between her and Tyler. Tonia hinted that there was no way a man and a woman not related could be so close and never consider the possibility of dating one another. Not the closeness that Elisha and Tyler shared anyway.

Tonia noted that neither one of them ever once referenced that the other was like a "brother" or "sister". And they each had something negative to say whenever the other would get into a relationship like, "I think you're settling or you deserve to be treated better." Tonia, a sociologist by trade, presumed herself to be an expert in relationships ever since obtaining her license in counseling, but Elisha reminded her that there was only one expert and His name is God. Tonia had smirked at her comment, but humbly corrected herself by stating instead that she was a professional.

"And what are you all dressed up for?" Tonia asked, pointing at Elisha's sassy pointed toe heels.

Elisha giggled as she opened her coat and showed off the rest of her outfit. The dress was a basic A-line, but with her accessories she made the ensemble fit for a classy affair. "Will has a company celebration dinner at that nice restaurant in town."

"His company?"

"Yes, you remember I told you that he's an independent contractor."

"That's right, you did."

"Anyway, he invited his guys out tonight to show them a good time since work has been slow. He wanted to celebrate the new upcoming project here in town. You know about the new real estate development downtown."

"Yeah, I heard about it on the news."

"Well, Will's company won a bid to be one of the subcontractors."

"Wow, that's great. I've been hearing that it's a big deal bringing more jobs to the area. I think Rich said that a cousin of his will be working on the site too. They're supposed to be breaking ground in a couple weeks."

"Yeah, Will said that he's excited about it even though he lives a town over. You know he can practically work anywhere as a certified electrician, but he'd rather be close to me. And this job couldn't have come at a better time."

"Oh, that's wonderful, Elisha." Tonia sounded somewhat skeptical. "So, will he be commuting?"

"Yes," Elisha answered, oblivious to the suspicion grounded on Tonia's face. "It's only a forty-five minute drive from where he lives. So, it's doable." She sat down on the loveseat near the crackling fireplace. "It's even better for his crew being that some of them live even closer than he does."

"Sounds like a win-win situation, especially since you guys will be able to see more of each other."

"I know. *So*, how do I look? He wanted me to wear something nice."

Tonia blinked from the hopeful gaze on Elisha's face and smiled. "The fashion queen wants *my* advice on clothes? Please, you are *workin'* that dress," Tonia complimented her friend with a snap of her fingers. "Humph, I can't wait to get back in the gym and get rid of this baby weight. You're making me look bad." She giggled while glancing down at her stomach and thighs.

"You'll be back to your old self in no time. I mean look at you, you've barely gained any weight at all."

"Stop the madness, girl. I know you're just trying to be nice." Tonia waved her off. "Between listening to my smart mouth little sister ask why I haven't been wearing the corset to make my stomach go down and my cousin, Eileen, telling me that I'm big, I almost lost it on them."

"But you just had a baby," Elisha justified.

"Try telling them that, they don't care." Tonia laughed as she plopped down on the sofa across from Elisha. "It's okay though. The fact that I can't fit my old clothes yet lets me know that I need to lose some weight. I'm not blind. I just remind them that I have a reason and ask what their excuse is."

Both Elisha and Tonia broke out into unified laughter.

"That's a good one," Elisha quipped. "But for real girl, you look good for having a six-week-old."

"Seven weeks tomorrow," Tonia specified. "Can you believe that she is almost two months old?"

"Wow, time is flying. I can't wait to have kids." A glow radiated Elisha's face.

"Uh, yes you can." Tonia gave her the wary eye with a dismissive grunt. "Do you see these bags?" Tonia pointed underneath her eyes. "Compliments of my little bundle of joy."

"Girl, you are too much." Elisha giggled. "Where is that little bundle of joy anyway?" She looked around the room, noticing the empty bassinet.

Tonia grabbed a white diaper cloth from the end table beside her and pointed down a hallway. "She's in the back with her grammy. Just went down for a nap. I could use one myself."

"I thought she watches the baby at night so that you can get some sleep."

"She does," Tonia yawned. "It's just my body adjusting back to my work schedule. Besides, I still have to pump milk for her. You know I do both bottle and breast feeding."

"That's right." Elisha nodded in remembrance. "Well, I guess I better let you get settled in for the night. I'll talk to you later." She then started for the door.

"Is everything okay?" Tonia stood and took a few steps behind Elisha. "I know that you didn't make a trip all the way over here to see Brianna on a Tuesday night when you have a dinner date in the opposite direction. Not to mention that we all plan to hang out this weekend when Jaleesa comes to town. Come on now, what's up?"

With a disquieted tone, Elisha admitted, "Yeah, there is something." She slowly walked back towards the sofa and sat down again.

"What is it?" Tonia carefully touched Elisha on the shoulder.

"I'm not really sure about things with Will." She peered up at Tonia and sighed. "I'm excited for him getting this bid, but I sort of feel …" Elisha wrung her hands. "I don't know."

"I thought you said you've been seeing him since last year. I mean, I don't blame you for keeping it a secret until you were sure about the relationship, but now that you've told everybody you're having second thoughts?"

"I know … crazy, right?" Elisha looked to her friend for understanding.

Tonia took a seat across from Elisha again and gently smiled. "Are you sure this has nothing to do with Tyler?"

Elisha pressed her lips together, desperately trying to conceal her emergent smile. "I don't know. He's different … in a good way. Not that he was bad or anything before. It's just that after two years of not seeing each other, and then that kiss—"

"*Kiss?*" Tonia leaned forward, pushing her long braids to the backside of her shoulder. "Wait a minute. You didn't say anything about a kiss."

Elisha bashfully looked away before she told Tonia everything about the afternoon with Tyler. She admitted that something clicked when they kissed for the first time, but challenged by the fact that she had already committed herself to someone else. Tonia shook a finger at her, reiterating her analysis of their friendship.

"I told you so." Tonia grinned.

"Yeah, you did. So, do you think that I should see where things could go with us? I mean, what do you think I should do?"

Tonia shook her head and groaned. "First of all, I'm biased. I know Tyler. He's always been cool with me. This Will guy, I don't know anything about him. Tyler reminds me of my husband, and that says a lot," Tonia boasted. "Rich cooks, cleans, and shows me *plenty* of attention and I've seen Tyler do the same. He has cooked for you on many occasions. When you lived in that apartment, I remember how he washed your car and let's not get started about the phone calls to make sure you got home safely after we all used to hang late at the Waffle House. The boy has been showing you for years that he'd rather be with you than those girls he dated." Tonia snapped her fingers with an attitude which caused Elisha to grin. "Bottom line, this is a decision you have to make for yourself. I am not going to be the blame if it doesn't work out."

"Oh, *now* you're all concerned about being the blame. Just a couple days ago you were ready to push us down the aisle," Elisha countered.

Tonia laughed, and then pointed at her. "I hear you, but that was just to get you to see what I saw a long time ago. Don't you remember when we all made lists about what we wanted out of a man? Me, you, Jaleesa, and Gina?"

Elisha nodded as she reviewed her list almost every day. It was a permanent bookmark in her study Bible.

"Okay, we all pretty much listed the same things. There were a few variations here and there, especially with Gina—"

"Yeah, she was always a little different." Elisha shook her head with a slight chuckle.

"But for the three of us, at least the top four things we all wrote in ink we said were non-negotiable." Tonia took a brief pause and then asked, "Do you still have yours?"

"Yes, I do."

"I know the kind of man Tyler is, but how does Will measure up?" Tonia raised a brow. "Don't answer me, just think about that." She then turned her head toward the hallway where her mother-in-law had suddenly appeared.

"Did she wake up?" Tonia asked about her baby.

"Oh no, she's still asleep. I just came out for a bite to eat," Mrs. Estman answered. She then glanced at Elisha before looking back to Tonia. "Oh, I didn't know you had company."

"Hi, Mrs. Estman. It's nice to see you again."

"Hello, Elisha. How are you?"

"I'm fine. I was just leaving." Elisha stood and told Tonia, "I don't want to be late." She quickly started for the door.

"Okay." Tonia walked closely behind her and said, "I'll be here if you want to talk."

Elisha nodded, quickly waved to Mrs. Estman, and then walked to her car.

She sat behind the wheel and offered a simple, yet sincere prayer to the Lord for Him to direct her path. She loved God and wanted to please Him above anyone or anything else. Despite her misgivings, it was time for Elisha to *listen* to God's answer. She had justified for so long what and who should be in her life without checking with the Lord first if that's what or who *He* wanted for her. He saved her life when she was terribly beaten and confidently placed her back on her feet.

She owed God everything, but in the midst of her prayer Elisha realized that she wasn't giving Him what He deserved. In order for her to receive a blessing she now understood that she would have to love the Giver more than the gift. As much as she wanted a husband, she wanted God more. After her prayer, Elisha felt a calm come over her. She wasn't agitated, nervous, or angry anymore. She was simply happy.

Although Elisha had chosen to ignore what her heart had felt for years, it was time to face the truth and discard the notion of compromise. God had given her confirmation, she was sure of it. And with His validation, her decision was made.

Chapter Eleven

"You look great," Will greeted Elisha in the parking lot of a neighborhood bar and grill. "I'm glad you could make it here on such short notice." He closed her car door after she stepped outside, and then hugged her around the waist. "Sorry again for changing the restaurant and not being able to pick you up." He carefully took her hand.

"Oh, that's okay. It works out better this way anyway. My mother called and I have to stop by my parents' house before going back home." Elisha dropped his hand and adjusted the straps of her purse. "Besides, I wanted to be here to help you celebrate." She pointed the remote on one of her key rings at the car and locked the door. "So, where's your car?" She looked around to find his vehicle in a sea of cars.

"Oh, it's parked right over there." Will pointed to the left where his car was parked just beneath a street light. "But come on, everybody is at the bar." He grabbed her hand again. "Let me introduce you."

"*At the bar?*" Elisha questioned. "I thought you were just meeting me here so that we could ride together to the other restaurant."

"No, girl." Will stared at her and then chuckled. "You have such a funny sense of humor. We're eating here." He squeezed her hand. "I know this is not what you had in mind, but the general contractor on a job I was working didn't pay like he was supposed to *so* …"

"Oh." Elisha's eyes drifted in another direction.

"But come on, we'll still have a good time here. I promise."

Elisha walked slightly behind Will as he led her by the hand inside the building. She reluctantly sat on a bar stool as Will introduced her to three guys and three other females whom she found out to be their girlfriends. He explained that there were others who worked with him, but the three men who were present have been with him faithfully for the past five years.

"These guys are trustworthy and loyal. And they know their jobs inside and out," Will complimented his employees.

"It's nice to meet you all." Elisha smiled and swiveled the stool away from the bar and in the direction that overlooked the restaurant.

"Order anything you like." Will slid a menu on the counter.

Elisha looked back at him, and asked, "Aren't we going to sit at a table? I figured you were at the bar just waiting for a table to become available." She cringed at the thought of anyone from her church seeing her at the bar.

"No, I like hanging at the bar. Besides, my two favorite teams are playing tonight." He pointed at a flat screen mounted overhead.

Elisha faced the bar again and looked up at the television to find two college basketball teams battling it out on the court. She then looked at the other people who were seated in a row on the opposite side of Will and inwardly grunted. *I got dressed up for this?*

"So, what'll you have?" the bartender asked Elisha.

"Another beer for me," Will spoke instead, and then looked to his girlfriend. "Babe, what'll you have? You know what, let me guess. You look like a strawberry daiquiri kind of girl." He pointed at her as if he was reading her mind. Before Elisha had a chance to respond, Will immediately looked back at the bartender and ordered, "Another beer and a strawberry daiquiri."

"Coming right up." The bartender tapped the wooden counter between them and quickly walked away.

Elisha glared at Will who seemed oblivious to her annoyance with him. "You drink?" She leaned in closer to keep their conversation somewhat private.

"Every now and then," Will flippantly replied. "Why, what's wrong with that?"

"Well, I don't." She widened her eyes at him.

"*Okay*, kudos to you. It's not a big deal. I'll just cancel the daiquiri and have him make it a virgin cocktail." He nonchalantly called the bartender back over and adjusted the order.

Elisha pressed her lips tightly together, angered by the fact that he drank and also by the assumption he made that she was a drinker too. In no uncertain terms did she ever say or lead him to believe that she drank alcohol of any kind. In fact, she has never touched the stuff. Not even in her unsaved days.

Will pointed at the television with the new bottle of beer nestled between his fingers, and hollered, "Ah, I think my bet is about to pay off! I hope you guys are ready to cough up that fifty bucks!"

Great, he's loud and gambles too.

Elisha rolled her eyes, embarrassed that she had been such a bad judge of character. She couldn't believe that Will had changed so much. As she stared at him, he was no longer the man who made her feel like she was floating on a cloud. Her stomach wasn't fluttering at the sound of his voice, and she definitely regretted telling her friends about him. His behavior tonight made her decision to break it off with him that much easier.

After leaving Tonia's house, Elisha had decided to give Tyler a chance. She realized that everything she truly wanted out of a man, he epitomized. And as she looked at Will, Elisha was happy that she had made the right decision. It wasn't about comparing the two men. It was about recognizing the one who had been in front of her all along.

Tyler's heart was sincere for the Lord; that she had known for a while. He was financially independent, to the point that he was debt free and even periodically paid bills for his mother. They've been friends since grade school, so she knew that he didn't have any children. If he had during the time they were out of contact, his mother would have been the first to show pictures off at the school. The only thing she wasn't sure of was his flair for romance.

Elisha cut her eyes away from Will and shook her head. The more she thought about Tyler, the more she was ready to tell him that she wanted to take their friendship to a relationship. That was until her eyes landed on him seated in a booth with another woman.

Chapter Twelve

As Tyler sat in a booth engrossed in a conversation with another woman, Elisha's eyes narrowed to a squint. She watched as he moved his folded hands from the table when a waitress approached, carrying two large plates. Elisha stared in disbelief as she fought to blink back her tears. It wasn't until the moment after she prayed to God that she realized she loved this man in *that* way.

"Hey, are you all right?" Will asked, lightly touching her arm. "You don't look well."

"No, actually I'm not feeling very well." She avoided eye contact with him. "Listen, I think I better go." Elisha grabbed her purse from the back of the barstool and stood.

"Are you sure? Can I get you something?" Will abandoned his bottle of beer and stood beside her.

"*No* ..." Her eyes discreetly drifted back to where Tyler and another woman were seated.

Elisha watched as the woman stood and pecked Tyler on the cheek before disappearing to a dimly lit hallway at the back of the restaurant.

"What is it?" Will's eyes followed hers.

Elisha snapped from her gaze. "I just need to get out of here."

"Oh, okay. At least let me walk you out." He took her hand like he had when she first arrived.

Elisha snatched her hand away. "Don't do that, I said that I was okay. You stay here and entertain your friends." She waved her hand in the air and rolled her eyes away from him.

Will stared at her, careful to keep his distance.

"I'm sorry," she apologized, quickly realizing her outburst. "I just have to go."

"Okay, that's fine … I'll call you later tonight."

"Yeah, sure." Those were her last words before she rushed out of the restaurant.

Elisha hurried behind the wheel to her car and slammed the door shut. She looked back at the restaurant where Tyler was seated next to a large glass window. He stood as the female returned to the table and then sat down again once she was in her seat. *Chivalry isn't dead.*

The woman's flowing long hair bounced on her shoulders as she adjusted herself in the seat. She was petite, a similar build to Elisha. Her skin tone was an almond brown and her clothes of the latest fashion. The navy canvas tote with a medallion bearing the MK emblem on the seat next to her matched the designer wedge pumps on her feet. She was attractive, just the kind of woman Tyler would go for.

Elisha shook her head as she pulled the cell from the side of her purse. She dialed Tyler's number and stared at him once the phone started ringing. She watched as he held up a forefinger to his date and walked away from the table.

"Hello?" His voice low, his tone puzzled.

"Hey, what's going on? I haven't heard from you in a few days."

"Uh, hey Elisha. Well, I've been kind of busy with my mother. Remember she had the surgery yesterday."

"Oh." Elisha paused. After a few seconds of silence, she asked, "So, how is she?"

"She's coming along. Still in the hospital recovering, but she'll be home in a few days."

"Well, that's good." Elisha gazed into the restaurant, trying to see where he had gone. "Are you at the hospital now?"

"No, I'm not. I had been there since yesterday morning until this evening. I decided to sleep at home tonight. You know, to get a break."

"Oh … are you at home now?"

"Uh no, I'm not…" Tyler sighed. "Was there something you needed?"

"I was just calling because I found the card you wrote and wanted to know if we could talk about it."

"Oh, you're just now finding it?" he sarcastically questioned.

"No, but I've been thinking. Can we talk?" Elisha buried her eyes on the woman he had left seated in the booth. "I really want to see you." Elisha gritted her teeth while watching the woman nibble from the plate on the other side of the table. "How about now?" she dared to ask.

"*Now*?" Tyler's voice went up an octave.

"Yes, unless you're busy." She toyed with him.

"Well, I am kind of in the middle of something right now. How about tomorrow?"

Elisha's nostrils flared as she took the phone from her ear and ended the call. There weren't any pleasantries of saying I'll be waiting, no problem, or even good-bye. She just hung up and threw her phone onto the passenger seat. She backed out of her parking space and looked through the restaurant's large glass window and watched as Tyler rejoined the woman in the booth. *He didn't even try to call back.* Livid, she sped out of the parking lot and onto the highway.

Moments later, Elisha's cell began to ring again. She shamelessly smirked, figuring that it was Tyler calling her back. She reached over for the phone and stared at the screen. Her smile faded as she saw that it was her sister, Charity.

"Hello." Elisha's tone was flat and dry.

"Well hey. Are you busy?" Charity asked.

Elisha bypassed answering her question, and snapped, "I thought you were supposed to call me last night."

"Uh hello, last night I was on the phone with my *fiancé*," Charity explained. "Milton can be longwinded when he's ready. He wanted to tell me about his day and would not let me get off the phone until I told him about mine." She giggled, taking on Elisha's usually chipper tone. "Not to mention that we have a wedding to plan in like no time."

Elisha sucked her teeth, and then sourly mumbled, "Whatever."

"*Whatever*? What's going on with you?" Charity's tone changed to match her sister's.

"Charity look, I'm not feeling well. I really have to go. I'll call you tomorrow." Elisha then hung up on her too.

Stopped at a traffic light, Elisha hit the steering wheel with the bottom of her hand and screamed. Her phone started ringing again. She waited until Charity's call went to voicemail and then turned the phone off.

With conflicting and mixed emotions, Elisha had more than enough to think about tonight. And the last thing she wanted to hear more of was another happy couple getting married. At least not right now.

Chapter Thirteen

Autopilot, that's what Elisha operated on for the past three days after seeing Tyler on a date with another woman. She had successfully avoided Charity, Tonia, and her mother's phone calls since Tuesday night. The only person she had willingly spoken to was Will.

"Elisha Maxwell, how may I help you?" she answered her direct line at work.

"You can help me by responding to my voicemail and texts," Tonia demanded. "I have been worried about you. You never called after your date on Tuesday. And last night when I texted you to ask if we were still on for tonight, you didn't respond. So, I figured I better call your job before I got your mother involved."

Elisha shook her head with a slight smirk on her face. "Really Tonia, you would call my mother as if I'm sixteen years old? I am a grown woman." She chuckled, the complete opposite from the woman who was practically falling to pieces a few nights prior.

"Well Ms. Grown Woman, what has been going on with you? Is everything all right?"

"Tonia, calm down. If you were really that worried, you would have driven to my house last night."

Tonia released a faint snigger. "I know, I know. But girl, that baby of mine had me up late and I was too tired to even talk. That's why I sent a quick text. And I even fell asleep twice while I was doing that!" She laughed.

Elisha nodded as she swiveled her chair around to face the window overlooking a wooded area just beyond the back street of the school. "I see how much you care." She chuckled, noticing an unauthorized vehicle parked on the road normally used for buses only. "But seriously, everything is fine. I was just taking some time for myself. I had a lot of thinking to do." She stood and stared to see if anyone was inside of the dark colored car.

"Oh yeah? So, when are you going to let Tyler know that you want him to be your man?" Tonia sounded convinced.

"No need … I chose Will." Elisha walked closer to the window and tried to figure out the make and model of the car, but the tail lights lit up and it was soon out of sight.

"*Will?* But I thought—"

"I know what you *thought*." Elisha sat back down at her desk and scribbled a note to herself on a yellow legal ruled pad. "But after really thinking some things through, I decided to see where things will go with us."

"Are you sure? I mean, have you spoken to Tyler since that night he was at your house?"

"Nope," she bluntly replied, tossing aside the pencil she had just used. "Not unless you count fifteen seconds on the phone while he was on a date with another woman a conversation. Yes, I saw him that night after leaving your house."

"What?" Tonia's voice was laced with confusion. "Did you two talk? Did you ask him who the woman was?"

"I really didn't need to. He showed me how much he really wanted to be with me by telling me that he had to call me later. Just like some other guys I've dated, him saying that he wanted to be with me was all talk."

"Really? Why would he do that? Tyler has always been straight with you. Do you think he wrote you that letter just to mess with your head? No, that's not him."

"How do you know what's him? Oh, I forgot, you're trying to analyze our friendship again."

"No, I'm just trying to find out why you would say something like that because—oh never mind."

"What?"

"Never mind."

"Tonia, what did you do?"

"It wasn't my idea."

Hesitant in her response, Elisha questioned, "What idea?"

After a sigh, Tonia admitted, "Rich saw Tyler in the grocery store last night and they sort of talked."

"Yeah … *and?*"

"And he told him that his mother was in town until Sunday afternoon and Tyler told him that his mother won't be released from the hospital until Monday. *So* … they want to get together tonight."

"And what does that have to do with me? I thought us girls were just hanging tonight. At least that's what we all planned last week. Jaleesa is coming in town today."

"Well, I just talked to her. We're all getting together tomorrow instead of tonight. Besides, she really wanted to go out with her fiancé tonight. So, I thought that you, Tyler, Rich, and I could have sort of a double date. Rich wanted to catch up with him before he left town and since Gina said something came up last minute at work."

"Oh, *you* thought." Elisha sighed as she glanced back at the road behind the school before she sat down and faced her desk.

"Look, I can tell him and Rich to just go out alone and then we can hang."

Elisha rolled her eyes as she toggled the mouse to her computer. As the screensaver disappeared, she saw an email from Will in her inbox. She skimmed through the message and rested against the back of the chair.

"So, I'll just call Rich now."

"No, don't do that," Elisha quickly spoke. "Since Gina and Jaleesa are so tied up with their busy schedules, I'll just come by your house later."

"Oh … okay." Tonia sounded surprised. "Are you sure? You just said that you chose Will."

"Yes, I'm sure." Elisha kept her eyes glued to the computer screen. "Besides, it's not a double date. Tyler and I have been friends forever. It'll just be old friends hanging out."

"Now you're old friends again? So, this rift between y'all isn't affecting your *friendship* in any way now?"

"We're two grown adults. I can handle myself."

"Okay …" Tonia now sounded skeptical. "I'll tell Rich and we can all just meet at our house. It'll be good to get out this weekend. Especially since Mrs. Estman is leaving soon. I am going to enjoy this little break because it'll be full-time Mommy-hood once she goes back home." She chuckled.

Elisha briefly looked away from the computer and glanced at the clock on her wall. "Is six-thirty okay?" She tapped her fingernails on the desk.

"Six-thirty is perfect. I'll be home by a quarter after five. That'll give me time to shower, change, and kiss and feed the baby."

"Okay, well let me tie things up here and I'll see you then."

"Okay, girl. See you later."

Elisha hung up and stared back at the email Will had sent her an hour ago. He had canceled the private dinner date they had planned for tonight because his daughter was sick and wanted to see her daddy. It would've been a chance for her to see if he could cook half as well as Tyler, but she had to take the back seat to his child. Tonia didn't know it, but Elisha was going to flake on her just as their other friends, Gina and Jaleesa, had.

Confused that he chose to email instead of calling her, Elisha questioned whether or not he was even telling her the truth.

With her fingers poised over the keyboard, Elisha paused with a sigh. She then quickly replied to Will that she hoped his daughter felt better and that she would check in with him tomorrow. After she sent the message, Elisha shook her head noting that her decision to be with him had left her again with second thoughts. He wasn't the man she wanted, but reasoned that at least she wasn't single anymore. *Why does it have to be so hard, Lord?*

Elisha hadn't been raised to compromise on what she really wanted in life; especially on something as important as a potential husband. At this point in her life, she wasn't interested in simply dating just to date. She was tired of the singles scene. She wanted someone to come home to at night—the same someone to wake up to in the morning. Elisha craved to have that special someone to share her hopes and dreams with, not a casual fling to disrupt her peace. She wanted someone who would truly love her like Christ loved the Church.

It wasn't in her to be satisfied with having a piece of a man to justify not having a man at all. As her desperation wore thin, those words sounded so ridiculous to her, but that's exactly how she was behaving. She had to make some solid decisions in her life to get what she wanted, and that's exactly what she was determined to do tonight.

Another Friday afternoon concluded her work week and Elisha gathered her things to leave. She turned the lights out to her office, and with a renewed mission confidently exited the building.

Chapter Fourteen

It was as if time stood still when Tyler walked through the doors of the restaurant. The crowded place suddenly went silent as butterflies fluttered in Elisha's stomach. Despite how confident she felt wearing one of the fiercest outfits she owned, her nerves tried to get the best of her. Elisha swallowed the excess moisture in her mouth as Tyler approached the table where she, Tonia, and Rich were seated. Her eyes drifted in another direc-tion as he shook hands with Rich and greeted Tonia with a warm hug.

"Good evening, sir," a waitress welcomed Tyler before he took his seat. "I just took drink orders. What would you like?"

Tyler casually smiled with the woman and answered, "Water is fine."

She nodded and then quickly walked away.

Elisha dared to look in his direction as Tyler simply raised a forefinger to acknowledge her presence. She quietly said hello, wondering why he chose not to meet up at Tonia and Rich's house like she had.

"So Tonia, Rich here tells me that you're a natural when it comes to motherhood." Tyler grinned as he took a seat at the round table.

"Aw, he said that." Tonia endearingly looked at her husband and smiled. She kissed him on the cheek and lovingly cleared the lipstick residue from his face.

"Yes, he did. When we talked last night it was like he couldn't stop saying how blessed he was to have a woman like you in his life."

"Oh honey," Tonia whispered to Rich. "That is so sweet."

"Well, it's the truth," Rich continued, flattering his wife. "That's why I married you."

Tyler grinned, and then met eyes with Elisha who wore a faraway gaze.

"Here you are, sir." The waitress returned with a glass of water and placed it in front of Tyler.

His concentration broke from Elisha as he said, "Thank you," to the waitress.

"Do you all need a few moments before placing your orders?" the waitress asked.

Each of them glanced at the other while shaking their heads.

"No, I think we're all ready," Tonia spoke up. "Unless you need more time, Tyler."

"No, this is my favorite place. I practically have the menu memorized." He then stared at Elisha when he added, "I already know what I want."

Tonia made a face at her husband that defied explanation. With a telling smirk on her face, she brushed the nape of her neck and said, "All righty then."

Elisha tried not to blush, wondering what kind of game Tyler was trying to play with her. He watched her movements carefully as the waitress scribbled down the orders and walked away. When she returned his stare he looked down to his buzzing phone.

"Oh, excuse me," he said, and then peered up at everybody. "I have to take this. I'll only be a minute."

Tonia and Rich nodded while Elisha questioned, "Who is it?"

Tonia shot Elisha a glare that would have ordinarily caused her to take notice, but not tonight. Elisha pressed on with a raised eyebrow, "Your girlfriend?"

A wave of confusion floated across Tyler's face as he stood.

"Is it the woman you were out with a few nights ago?" Elisha relentlessly interrogated.

Tyler glanced at Rich and then to Tonia who declared, "That's enough. Come with me outside."

Tonia took Elisha by the hand and pulled her out of the restaurant into the parking lot. "What are you doing?" she questioned as they neared her SUV. "You are making yourself look desperate, you know."

"So you're on his side now?" Elisha's arms flopped to her sides as if in defeat.

"What are you talking about? You just told me today that you didn't want him. And now you're up here flirting like this is some game."

"Well, isn't that how Gina got Michael to see what he was missing?"

"Number one, Gina is not saved," Tonia scoffed. "Okay. Sure, she's our friend, but she's on some other stuff. I try to tell her that going to church does not make her all right with God. Accepting Jesus as her Lord and Savior does. But of course you know if I tell her that, then I'm judging. But anyway." Tonia rolled her eyes. "You on the other hand, know better. You have everything going for you."

"Tonia, how can you say that? You're the one with a husband and a child. You're the one who is living the life that I want. You can't stand there and tell me what it's like to be single when you have a man in your bed every night!" Elisha's eyes watered as she vented. "I am so sick and tired of listening to married women acting like it is so easy to live this life that I'm living."

"Let me tell you something, I never said that it was easy." Tonia pointed at her. "For crying out loud, Elisha, Rich and I have had our fair share of ups and downs. Don't get me wrong, he is a good man, I won't take that away from him, but he isn't perfect. To even get to the point of being married took work. It was not easy. Do you think that I didn't have urges to be with him before we were married? Do you think that I was just up in church every week for show? I was praying to God to keep me. There were times when I just wanted to let it all go. But I kept hearing that Voice say 'hold on'… Oh, we went through, girl, *but God*. So, don't go listening to Gina, she doesn't know the meaning of hold on when it comes to that."

Elisha laughed through her tears.

"Seriously." Tonia managed to calm Elisha with her words. "Gina justified sleeping with Michael before they were married by saying, 'we're *going to* get married.' And it got even worse once she had the engagement ring. I couldn't even stand to listen to her anymore. Up there justifying that it was okay because the wedding plans had been made."

Tonia flipped her long braids to her back and then placed a hand on Elisha's shoulder. "Honey look, you're just having a weak moment, and God knows this, so just hold on like He said. Be patient and listen to what He has placed in your heart. You know that He'll never steer you wrong."

Elisha nodded as Tonia hugged her.

Tonia reached into her front pocket of her jeans and pulled out a piece of tissue. "Now take this and clean yourself up."

"Tonia, I can't go back in there." Elisha shook her head as she dabbed the tissue underneath her eyes. "Not like this. I'm a mess." She then sat on the back bumper of Tonia's truck.

Tonia sat beside her and nudged Elisha with her shoulder. "Hey listen, I'm sorry. I guess I should've never asked you to come to this date night thing. Looks like it just opened a whole can of worms that weren't ready to come out."

Elisha shrugged. "No, that's not your fault. Some things were bound to come out. The truth is that I wanted to see Tyler ... I love him, Tonia," she honestly admitted. "I'm in love with my best friend." She chuckled between her sniffles. "*Wow*, who knew?"

"Uh, I knew." Tonia raised a hand.

The two of them broke into laughter.

"I tell you what, I'll go back in there and let them know you're not feeling well. Rich and I can take you home. You need some time to sort through things. And you definitely need some time alone with Tyler."

"Are you sure? I can just sit out here until you guys finish dinner." Not even Elisha could keep a straight face when she uttered those words.

"Girl please, you know you're not going to sit out here by yourself while we're in there eating." Tonia giggled. "Anyway, I'll go get the keys. You sit tight and I'll be right back."

"Okay. And please get my coat and purse for me." She folded her arms.

"I will. And don't worry. Rich is used to purse duty." Tonia laughed as she waved a hand in Elisha's direction.

Elisha smiled as she watched Tonia walk back towards the double doors leading inside of the restaurant. She then stood from the bumper and slowly paced a small area surrounding Tonia's truck. Elisha casually waved at a few patrons who walked past her to get to their vehicles and fidgeted with the jeweled ribbon that hung from her necklace. It was cold and she was ready to go home.

Just then she saw Tyler walking in her direction, carrying her coat draped across his arm and her purse clutched uncomfortably in his hand. She smiled to herself because he was just the person she wanted to take her home.

Chapter Fifteen

"So, are you going to tell me what's going on with you?" Elisha asked Tyler as he pulled out of the restaurant's parking lot.

Tyler straightened his posture as he kept his eyes glued on the road.

"Uh, hello? I know you hear me talking to you." She folded her arms across her chest and stared at him.

"Yeah, I hear you." Tyler glanced at her and cracked a smile. "What do you want to know, Elisha?"

"Don't act cute with me." She managed to snatch the smile off his face. "For starters, how are you going to leave a letter like that in my house and then get with some other woman?" She belabored the point. "Are you trying to play games with me?"

"Oh, here we go." Tyler clenched his jaw shut and looked away from her.

"I asked you a question."

"How am I playing games with you when you told me that you had a boyfriend?" Tyler raised his voice to match hers.

"So, your feelings just up and disappeared? It sure didn't take you long to move on," she huffed. "What is that about?"

"For one, I didn't give you that letter—"

"Oh, so is there some other woman named Elisha that you're in love with?"

"If you would let me finish." Tyler shook his head and sighed. "I didn't give you the letter again because you told me that you had a boyfriend. I had it out to give to you, but then we kissed and then you said you had a man, and I wasn't trying to be that guy."

"What guy?"

"The one trying to be with a woman who wants nothing to do with him."

"So, you just up and start seeing someone else?"

"Elisha, what do you expect me to do?" Tyler questioned her as they neared a traffic stop light. "I'm not some little kid. I'm a grown man who wants more than a fling. I want a *wife* … I wanted you!"

The silence after his confession caused his voice to linger in the air.

"See, this is what I did not want." Tyler grunted. "We never use to argue like this. Look, I'm just going to drop you off at home and call it a night before we both say something that we'll regret."

Elisha grunted and furiously looked away from him. In all of the years they had been friends, he's right, they never use to argue like this. They've had disagreements and debates about certain things, but now that intimate emotions were involved the parameters of their friendship had changed without notice.

Tyler pulled into Elisha's driveway. As he parked the car, he noticed the anger still etched on her face. Tyler knew her well enough to know that behind that rage was someone who had been hurt repeatedly over the years. And as much as he wanted her to see his side, Tyler didn't want things to end like this between them.

"Elisha, listen, … of course my feelings didn't just up and disappear." He nudged her chin in his direction. "The woman that I was out with is an old friend. We saw each other in passing and since I am single, I asked her out. It wasn't to get back at you or to play some childish game … it was just to move on."

Elisha nodded as she took her seatbelt off. Somewhat reserved in her approach, she questioned, "So, have you moved on?"

His eyes pierced hers with an electrifying connection as he asked, "Have you?"

"I tried to," she admitted with a smile, and then glanced away. "But I can't."

Tyler moistened his lips, confident as he spoke, "If you want me as much as I want you, why is that so hard to say?"

"Because…" Tears began to form in her eyes.

"Because what?" Tyler tenderly wiped them away.

"I didn't know how to tell you after I saw you with that woman."

Tyler removed his seatbelt and pulled Elisha closer to him. "You know you can tell me anything," he assured her. "I would never do anything to intentionally hurt you." He stroked the back of her head and whispered the words he had written to her in the letter, "I love you."

Elisha looked up and gazed into his brown eyes, recognizing that his words were true. She gripped his hands, squeezing his fingers tightly, and said, "I love you, too."

Chapter Sixteen

The sun poured through the cracks of the white wooden blinds of Elisha's living room. It cast a striped shadow across the furniture, a high school yearbook, and a glass bowl where popcorn kernels had settled at the bottom. The large flat screen TV mounted on the wall displayed the menu of a movie she and Tyler had fallen asleep on the night before. There were several waded pieces of tissue on the coffee table next to an open manila folder that contained photos and medical records from Elisha's assault the previous year.

As she stirred in his arms, Tyler's eyes opened. He looked down and smiled at Elisha sleeping partially on his chest as they lay nestled into the crevices of her white leather sofa. He looked above and whispered the words, "Thank you, Lord."

When Elisha heard the sound of his voice, her eyelashes fluttered. She stretched her arms across Tyler's body and yawned. She gazed up into his inviting eyes and smiled. "Hey, you."

"Hey." His deep morning voice serenaded her ears.

The two practically glowed in the purity of their bond. A relationship that started out as mere childhood friends had blossomed into best friends in love.

"Thank you for staying over. I'm glad we had a chance to talk." Elisha delicately traced the curvature of his jaw with her fingertips.

"Me too." Tyler softly kissed her on the forehead. "I didn't want to leave things like that between us. Even if we had decided not to get together, I wouldn't have felt right about us arguing like that. I mean, we have already spent two years not talking. And I definitely didn't want to go through that again."

Elisha's eyes drifted down as she fiddled with the buttons on his shirt. "So, are you sure that you want to do this?" she asked, making mention of the conversation they had the night before. "I know I laid a lot on you last night."

"You don't have to go over that again. That's a sorry excuse for a human being." He angrily scoffed. "What kind of man puts his hands on a woman like that? And those pictures and medical records ... You should have gone to the police. Nathan would have looked out for you. And you definitely should've told your mother. Since she was DA at the time, she would've definitely put him away."

"I know, but I was so embarrassed. I just couldn't face her. I couldn't even face Tonia."

"Well, you don't have to worry about that happening again. I'm here." He squeezed her shoulder.

Elisha gazed up into his eyes and said, "I know … to serve and protect, right?"

"Yeah, to serve and protect … and love," he tenderly responded.

"You know if we take that step we talked about … that's a permanent commitment for me." She then searched his eyes for a sign that his feelings were completely mutual.

"I feel the same way. You know I wouldn't take something like that lightly."

"I already knew that." Elisha kissed him on the cheek. "*So* … just let me pack my bag and make that phone call."

"You mean to Will?"

"Yep." Elisha scooted to an upright position and edged her way to the opposite side of the couch. "If we're going to be … well, *us*, he should be one of the first people to know." She stood and slid on her slippers.

"Oh, I agree. I just figured you'd call your mother or Charity, or even Tonia first." Tyler stretched his legs and propped his hands behind his head for a more comfortable position.

"No, I want to do this right. I never should have accepted him as my boyfriend when I wasn't fully committed to the idea of even being with him in the first place. And besides that, I knew in my heart what God was telling me."

"And what's that?"

She took a moment before responding, "Not to settle."

Tyler nodded knowingly. "I feel you. When I was out with Nadia—"

"Nadia?"

"The woman that I went out with earlier this week, that's her name."

"Oh."

"Well, when I was out with her, all I could think about was you. Don't get me wrong, if you didn't want me, I was going to move on, but I still felt that you were the one for me."

"Yeah, well, I'm glad you came after me." Elisha leaned over and kissed him on the lips.

"Baby, I love you and everything, but there's one thing that we both need to take care of before we go any further."

Bewildered, she asked, "And what's that?"

"The morning breath."

Elisha pushed him on the shoulder and popped him with a decorative pillow before heading to her bedroom.

"Hey, are you just going to leave me hanging?" Tyler stood and gestured with his hands. "I don't live here, remember? I know you have a spare toothbrush. You *always* have a spare for everything," he teased.

"Yeah, I guess I could help you out with that." She sashayed back in his direction. "But only because you're my man." She wrapped her arms around his neck and he kissed her on the cheek.

"*Mmm*," he moaned. "I like how that sounds."

Elisha inwardly praised God for answering her prayer. She almost allowed her impatience to ruin the opportunity to be with the man of her dreams. The fixation on getting married nearly trumped the process it took to get there. As she gazed into Tyler's eyes, Elisha knew that she was about to settle for Will when he didn't possess all of the qualities she truly desired in a mate. And knowing that now helped her to realize that if she had settled with Will their relationship would have been doomed for failure.

"There's extra tooth paste, tooth brushes, and soap in the guest bedroom."

"Soap? What are you trying to tell me?" He sniffed underneath his arms. "Hey, I took a shower before we met up last night."

"You know what I mean." Elisha laughed at his comical nature. "I was just letting you know."

"I know." Tyler winked.

"I'll be back in a minute." Elisha started in the opposite direction again.

"Breakfast? I can cook you something," he offered.

Pulled back by his sincerity, Elisha answered, "Sure." She then glanced at the clock that read eight-forty and it triggered her memory. "Oh no, shoot … I forgot that my mother is coming at ten."

"Wait," Tyler said with his eyebrows raised. "She's not coming *here*, is she?" He emphasized by pointing down.

"Yeah, why? Is that a problem?"

"Uh, yeah," he replied with a touch of sarcasm in his voice. "I think that we should ease into this thing. Remember, the last time I saw her was in court."

Elisha pondered his statement. "You're right … I'm sorry, I wasn't thinking."

"How about this, we have breakfast and I come back over later? I don't want to cause any tension right now. I want our plans to go smoothly." He stared her in the eyes. "We're still leaving at three o'clock, right?"

Elisha recalled their commitment and she nodded. "Yeah, at three. But…"

"But what?"

"I haven't gone grocery shopping this week. So, maybe we can just have lunch later after I've met with Mama."

"Girl, you're going to have to do better." Tyler chuckled. "Especially if you plan to get married."

"I'm not going to argue with you on that one," Elisha agreed. "I'll just grab some toast and orange juice. I think I still have some left in there."

Tyler shook his head at her. "I can go get you something."

"No, I'm fine. Besides, I'll probably just have brunch with Mama while we're out looking for things for Charity's wedding," she figured, and then said with a wink, "Let me run to the bathroom right quick so you can get a proper goodbye."

Tyler nodded with a smile on his face as he started in the opposite direction for the guest bathroom. When the two met up again, Elisha had already slipped into her bathrobe. They stood in the doorway and kissed as if it were the first time they had seen each other in years. Tyler stroked Elisha on the small of her back and she giggled from the tickle.

"You know that's my spot," she whispered in his ear.

"Now I do. I like learning new things about you." He nibbled on her neck.

"You better go." She nudged him away with a slight push on the chest. "I have to get ready or I'll never hear the end of it from my mother."

"Okay." He squeezed her shoulders. "I'll see you in a few hours then."

"Yeah … a few hours." Elisha took his hands, nursing their flirtatious behavior.

Their intertwined fingers temporarily coasted in the air before the increasing distance pulled them apart. Tyler walked to his car, noticing the vehicle across the street in the driveway.

"Your neighbors, I guess they make pretty good money, huh?" He gazed at the dark, tinted windows. "That Mercedes is nice."

"I guess. The wife is an engineer and the husband is the owner of a car dealership. He brings home a different car just about every week," Elisha replied, peering across the street. "But I think I've seen that one before. You're right, it's really nice." The polished rims and reflective shine on the car glistened in the sun. "Hmm, I guess they got back in town early. I figured they would have been gone until tomorrow evening."

Elisha rubbed the sides of her arms as she stood in her pink bathrobe and slippers.

"Get back inside," Tyler instructed her as he pointed. "It's cold out here, girl."

"Yes, sir," she joked, backing inside from the doorway. "I'll call you later."

"Okay." Tyler glanced back at the car again before he slid behind his wheel.

Elisha closed the door and floated back inside.

Chapter Seventeen

The chill from outside rippled through Elisha's body even after she had closed her front door. She vigorously rubbed her hands together and hurried to reset her thermostat a couple degrees warmer. After returning the bowl and drinking glasses to the kitchen she and Tyler had used the night before, Elisha picked up the folder that held terrible memories of her horrid past. She released a liberating breath and carried the folder along with a pair of her boots to her bedroom.

"*Hey, Tyler,*" Elisha sung his name after she answered the cordless phone that was on the chaise lounge in her bedroom.

"Hey," he said after a goofy chuckle. "I was trying to save your home number in my phone, but it ended up calling you instead."

"Uh huh." Elisha giggled as she tossed her boots into a nearby corner and dropped the folder onto her bed.

"Yeah … look, I know you have to get ready, so I'll let you go."

"Okay." Elisha beamed from ear to ear.

"Three o'clock," Tyler confirmed their date.

"Yes, I'll be ready at three. I'm not changing my mind."

"I know … but do me a favor and keep your phone on."

"Why?"

"Just in case I want to hear your voice again."

Elisha blushed. *"Bye, Tyler,"* she sung his name again. and then ended the call. She placed the phone on its base, picked up the folder again, and then walked through the bathroom to her closet.

Moments after securing the folder back in her closet, she wrapped her hair beneath a pink shower cap. Suddenly, Elisha heard a text alert signal from her cell phone. She glanced at the clock, knowing that her mother hated to be left waiting. If she wasn't dressed and ready to walk out the door when she arrived, Elisha was sure to hear a lecture.

Again, there was another alert signal from her phone, but she ignored it, figuring that it was just Tyler saying something sweet again. After pulling out an outfit from her walk-in closet just off of her bathroom, Elisha then heard her phone ringing. This time she dropped her clothes on a small bench and rushed through the bathroom back into her bedroom. She reached for her cell next to the remote on the nightstand to see if it may have been her mother calling instead of Tyler, but her phone beeped, alerting that she had missed the call. Elisha scrolled through her phone and surprisingly saw that she had several texts from Will.

The conversation they needed to have was inevitable. Elisha tightened the belt to her bathrobe and sat on the edge of her bed. She scrolled through her phone to see what Will had written.

I can't see u anymore, the first message read.

We need 2 talk. I owe u that, the next one stated.

Please answer. I want 2 explain, the third one detailed.

Elisha squinted, trying to figure out what had happened with Will in between the time his child got sick and this morning. She wondered if he saw her out with Tyler or if he just decided to get back with the mother of his child. Elisha's shoulders lowered in relief because either way, she had Tyler. And her relationship with him was what mattered now.

Elisha flinched as the phone began ringing in her hand. She exhaled a deep breath as she stared at the screen and answered Will's call.

"Hello?" she answered, figuring that his decision defied any legitimate explanation. In her mind's eye, there was nothing left to talk about. He had obviously made the choice to move on without her and she was absolutely fine with it.

"Hey, I guess you're wondering what my texts are all about."

"Uh, you think?"

"Okay, I guess I deserved that," Will conceded. "I can explain."

"I'm listening."

"It was about work," he passively admitted.

"Work?" Elisha sought clarification. "I tried calling you Wednesday *and* Thursday, Will, and heard nothing back. Nothing other than a text about having a private dinner with me last night that you cancelled through email."

"Aside from talking things over with Monica—"

"Oh, you were talking things over your child's mother … *again*?" Elisha scoffed. "I guess you're getting married again too. You know, I don't know why I was acting like you were such a great catch when you're no different from some of the other guys I've dated," she contended. "I guess you were just stringing me along to do what? To see how much you could hurt me this time?"

"Elisha, calm down," Will urged her. "It wasn't like that. I only considered working things out with her *after* I found out that the new bid I won on that job we had celebrated the other night was in jeopardy."

"In jeopardy? What are you talking about? What in the world does any of this have to do with work?"

"That's what I'm trying to tell you. The general con-tractor for Gregory's Development Company is the owner's son."

"*And?*" Elisha's eyebrows furrowed as she wondered what in the world he was trying to explain.

"And apparently he still has a thing for you. He says you two dated," Will tried to jog her memory. "Elisha, I'm going to be straight with you, it really got to me. I was ready to make this thing work between us, but I need this job. He threatened to fire my company if I continued seeing you. I'm sorry, but I have a child to support—"

"Wait," she abruptly stopped him. *"What are you talking about?* I never dated anyone with the last name of Gregory. Are you just trying to find a way out because you want to get back with your ex?" Anger swelled inside of her. "Let me tell you something, you don't have to, Will. It's okay because I was going to break up with you too. You just helped confirm that I don't have to settle!"

"*Settle?*" Will's voice changed from civil to belligerent as he flipped the script on her. "See, you females act like a man owes you the world."

"*Ha!*" Elisha sarcastically huffed. "No, a *real* man would just be willing to offer it. And for me, a *real* man would first know God."

"I don't know what you're talking about because I know God," Will defended himself.

"Knowing God and knowing *about* Him are two different things," Elisha debated, now with a hand on her hip. "Between your drinking, gambling, and cursing I've seen enough."

"What? I've never cursed at you."

"I didn't say that you cursed at me, I'm saying that you curse. I don't know why I didn't say anything about it at the time, but you know what? That's the least of the problems. You've never prayed with me, you've never offered a word of Scripture to encourage me, *and* you've never asked me anything about my walk with God. If that's what you consider *owing a woman the world*, then I feel sorry for Monica."

"I don't have to listen to this—"

Elisha abruptly ended the call with a touch of her screen as she mumbled to herself, "Nope, you sure don't." She tossed the phone on the bed and dismissively waved her hand in the air.

Just then, the phone started ringing again. Elisha stopped mid-stroll and walked back over to the other side of the bed where she had thrown her phone aside.

"You've got to be kidding me." Her eyes narrowed as she watched Will's number scroll across the screen. "Uh hello," Elisha answered, mystified as to why he was calling her back when he just said that he didn't have to listen to her.

"Despite your childish behavior, I'm just warning you to watch your back."

"Watch my back? Oh, are you threatening me now?"

"Elisha, you need to listen to me. I'm telling you—"

Elisha ended the call again, and then mumbled, "I don't need to hear anything else you have to say."

There was an eerie silence as she stood, wondering why she allowed this man to ever be a part of her life. Replaying in her mind the warning Will spouted, Elisha questioned her judge of character again. After he had suddenly announced his engagement to another woman, Elisha now recognized that Will should have never been allowed back into her life.

Suddenly, the doorbell chimed and she snapped from her daze. Elisha eased toward the window. With slow, deliberate movements she quietly moved a flap of the wooden blinds upward and carefully scanned her front yard. Her eyes shifted from left to right for any sign of life. The driveway was empty except for a couple, a man and a woman, walking away from her house carrying papers in their hands.

Elisha quietly exhaled as the evangelists canvased the neighborhood just as they had several weeks ago. She recalled previously reading a pamphlet that had been stuffed in her door when she was not at home. *Seek the Lord while He may be found*, the pamphlet candidly read. It was a Scripture that had previously prompted her to totally give her life to Christ, instead of portions of it. Elisha knew that the Lord required all of her, and whomever she decided to share her life with had to as well. She regretted ever second-guessing that God had already prepared someone, a soul mate, for her to share her life with.

Still unnerved by Will's unprovoked threats, Elisha double-checked all of her doors to ensure that they were locked. She lingered by the sliding patio door that was slightly ajar and stared outside at her back yard. All was quiet. Elisha pushed the patio door tightly closed and locked it.

Just as she was about to activate the alarm, her cell began to ring in her hand. This time the display read Unknown Caller. Elisha sucked her teeth and ignored the call. Her mother would be there soon. Instead of being riled over Will's stalker tendencies, she pushed the phone aside on the foyer table.

Since she had come clean with Tyler about Chauncey's abuse, Elisha decided that this would be as good a time as any to do the same with her mother after she picked her up this morning. Sharing her newfound love for Tyler and the truth about her bruises from last year would bring peace, relief, and closure.

Just as Elisha stood in front of the panel for her alarm to activate the system, a gloved hand snatched her to the floor from behind.

Chapter Eighteen

"Hey man, I need you to run some plates on a Mercedes," Tyler said as he stood behind the car parked in the neighbor's driveway across the street from Elisha's house.

He doubled back to her house to surprise her with breakfast, but as he parked, a gnawing suspicion ate away at him. Despite the fact that Elisha had explained the numerous vehicles her neighbors brought home on a regular basis, Tyler couldn't shake the unsettling feeling that something wasn't right about that car being there. And to see that the plates on the vehicle weren't dealer tags, he needed to find out exactly who they belonged to.

"Yeah sure, give me a minute," Nathan responded. "Okay, what's the plate number?"

Tyler relayed the details located on the license plate tag on the back of the vehicle. He stared at the neighbor's house which showed no sign of life and then across the street to Elisha's where he had just parked his car in the driveway again.

"Hey man, let me get back with you in a few minutes. I have to finish this complaint before Harris comes breathing down my neck again. I see him down the hall now."

"All right," Tyler answered, listening to the background sound of keys rattling away on a keyboard.

"Five minutes tops," Nathan assured him.

"No problem. I'll be waiting." Tyler stuffed the phone back into his coat pocket and peered through the tinted windows of the car before he walked back across the street.

With a medium-sized paper bag from a nearby fast-food restaurant, Tyler stood on Elisha's welcome mat and rang the doorbell. Nobody answered. He moved his ear closer to the door and listened for any sound of movement, but heard nothing. After several seconds, he walked back to his car and sat behind the wheel, figuring that she must be in the shower or somewhere in the house out of earshot where the doorbell could not be heard.

Tyler placed the brown paper bag on the passenger seat of his vehicle and waited. His eyes drifted to the slip of paper in his cup holder that Elisha had given him last night. Determined to solidify the plans they had made, Tyler pulled his phone out again and made another call.

"Hello," a deep baritone voice answered after a raspy cough.

Tyler initially hesitated, but then confidently spoke, "Hi, Mr. Maxwell, how are you?"

"I'm good," Gerald replied. "Who am I speaking with?"

"Oh, I'm sorry sir. This is Tyler ... Tyler Hampton."

"*Tyler*," his voice livened. "It's been a long time. How are you doing?"

"I'm doing well, sir."

"Glad to hear it, son."

Those words struck Tyler. The one in particular that he hoped would soon hold another meaning was *son*. Ever since he had accepted Christ into his life, Tyler viewed Gerald as his spiritual father. His friendship with Elisha had always been a close one, and along the way came a special bond he had formed with her father. Although he never saw Elisha as a sister, Tyler had viewed Gerald as the father he never had. Someone he could talk to, someone who opened his life to him, someone he now longed to call Dad.

"Thank you, sir," Tyler nervously said. "I know it's been a long time, but in light of what had happened before I left town, I wasn't sure how to approach you ... or your wife."

"That's water under the bridge, son. The past is the past." Gerald cleared his throat and continued, "I never thought you were that type of person," he assured him. "My wife was just doing her job. I know that it's hard not to take something like that personal. She's that tenacious lawyer that never wanted to create a conflict of interest scenario ... with any of her cases. Margaret had to be tough. She wasn't sure what to think when your name showed up in the case file, but all in all, justice prevailed."

Tyler smiled as he listened. There was a weight lifted as Gerald continued sharing what he thought about him as well as his family. Although he was away often when he went on tour to promote his Gospel albums, Gerald kept a good rapport with many of the townspeople. Many of whom were former classmates.

"As you know, Margaret and I went to school with several of your family members."

"Yes, sir. I sometimes go through my mother's yearbook," Tyler interjected, now more comfortable than he was when he first dialed Gerald's number.

"Well then, you've seen my afro shrink to a shameful spoiler kit," Gerald joked.

Tyler helplessly laughed.

"It's okay though. Margaret thinks it gives me character, but of course my children think I should just shave it all off and be done with it. Especially my youngest. She got jokes." Gerald spoke of his daughter, Joy. "But I digress ... I said all of that just to say that it's always nice to see familiar faces like your family, the people I went to school with. I'm glad that none of them treated me any differently after the trial. Now, things did seem a little strained as far as my wife was concerned, but understand we are one."

"I understand," Tyler replied. He wanted others to soon see him and Elisha in the same light—as one.

"And as I made that mindset clear to others," Gerald staunchly noted, "we've smoothed out more than our fair share of, let's say, misunderstandings."

Tyler could imagine the tests their marriage had endured due to Margaret's career as District Attorney in a town with people they had gone to school with. It was a blessing that Tyler's mother never said a cross word about the situation. When asked, she would always reply, "I'm praying to the good Lord." Her example was one he wanted to pass on to his own children, having learned what that truly means over the past few years.

"So, how's your mother?" Gerald sincerely asked. "I usually hear about how she's doing through Elisha since they work together."

"She's doing better."

"Better?"

"Yes, she had surgery earlier this week, but she's recovering nicely. That's why I came home for a couple weeks. I have to be there for her once she's released from the hospital Monday."

"Well, I'm glad you told me. I hadn't spoken to Elisha this week, so I had no idea. I'll have to get by the hospital sometime this evening to see her."

Tyler warmed at his kind gesture and offered his mother's room number.

"I'm glad you called, Tyler. I hate to cut this short, but I have to speak with my wife before she leaves the house. But don't be a stranger, please come by before you head back to Tennessee. When I'm in town, my cell is always on."

"Uh sir, before you go," Tyler quickly said. "I need to ask you something." The nervousness that had left his body returned. His mouth became moist as he prepared to ask the question that had been burning on his heart.

"Sure, what is it?"

"I know this may seem a little sudden, but Elisha and I … well, I wanted to ask for your daughter's hand in marriage."

At first there was complete silence, and then Gerald replied, "Hmm, Elisha's hand, huh?"

"Yes, sir."

"Have you prayed about this?" Gerald inquired.

"Oh yes," Tyler simply responded. "I wouldn't have approached you if I hadn't."

More silence invaded the conversation before Gerald said, "I was wondering how long it was going to take for you two to figure out that you belonged together."

Tyler released a hearty chuckle as a broad smile spread across his face.

"Tyler, it would be my honor if you married my daughter. I've always wanted her to end up with you. Of course, you have my blessing … *son*."

Those words solidified the plans he and Elisha had made. Tyler was sure that the rest of the world would view their decision as rushed and maybe a little crazy, but when it's right—it is right. There had never been another romantic interest that he has held in such high regard as Elisha. Even when he dated other women, Tyler often compared them to her. For him, she was the standard. And being that no one else measured-up, he refused to compromise for less.

"Let's get together and talk. I want all four of us to settle everything."

"All four of us?" Tyler repeated.

"Yes. You, me, Elisha, and Margaret," Gerald clarified. "As family, we try to resolve anything that may cast doubts. And since you plan on marrying my daughter, this is one thing that I would like for you—*us*—to do. Okay?"

"Okay … yes, sir." Tyler respected Gerald and agreed with him that they should all start with a clean slate. He never wanted to marry into conflict, and resolving things between him and Margaret once and for all would ensure that he doesn't.

After the deep conversation he had with Elisha last night, Tyler was sure he had forgiven Margaret and all the changes her interrogation had put him through. It was difficult because she had known him practically all his life. Tyler had completely come to recognize that regardless of what Margaret thought of him at that moment, he was not a criminal. And as he ended the call with Gerald, he was resolved to ensuring that she knew he was the man for her daughter.

Tyler grabbed the paper bag from his passenger seat and walked up to Elisha's front door again. The breakfast was getting cold and according to Gerald, Margaret was about to leave the house. She would be at Elisha's front door soon and Tyler wasn't prepared to talk with her just yet. He too agreed that the four of them should sit down and talk amicably in order to get their marriage off to a good start. That way just felt right.

"Come on, Elisha. Open up," Tyler mumbled under his breath as he shifted his weight from one foot to the other. He pressed the chimer again, hoping that she would hear it and open the door. After he pressed the button a third time with no answer, Tyler dialed her number and listened as it went to voicemail. His suspicion heightened. "What are you doing in there, girl? Open the door. I'm outside with breakfast," he left her a message.

As promised, Nathan's number scrolled across his cell phone screen. Tyler glanced back at the black Mercedes Benz as he answered his friend's call.

"Were you able to find out anything?" Tyler quickly asked.

"I sure did. Sorry it took so long."

"No, you're fine. Now tell me, does the car belong to Karen or Jim Knightly?"

"Neither, the name I have here is Chauncey McDan-iel."

Tyler gasped as his phone along with the paper bag he held plummeted to the ground.

Chapter Nineteen

"What do you want?" Elisha fearfully asked with tears in her eyes. "If you leave now, you won't get arrested." Her back was against the frame of her bedroom door as she pleaded for Chauncey to leave her home.

"Nah, you don't get to call the shots here." He arrogantly laughed. "And I know I won't get arrested. No one came looking for me after the last time I was here." He pointed his long forefinger, and then traced it along her jawline. "See, I've figured you out." He sporadically shifted his eyes from hers to various parts of her face, scrutinizing every detail. "You have it all together. Pretty, smart, successful … and come from a good *Christian* family," he mocked. "That's why I've never met your parents. I've barely said hello to your friends, but yet we were together for a year. And being that you have so much … hmm, what's the word I'm looking for … *pride* … I know that you'll keep this a secret too."

Elisha flinched as his finger moved down the side of her neck. "Please Chauncey, you don't want to do this," she cried.

His eyes zeroed back to hers. "Do what? Do the same thing that you let that guy do last night?" He confronted her.

"Wh-What?" Puzzled, Elisha stared at him.

"*Wh-what?*" he mocked her, curling his lips. "You know what I'm talking about. I was with you for over a year and couldn't stay the night because you're such the good little *Christian* girl, but you got some other man up in here all night long?"

Elisha's body stiffened as she realized that Chauncey had been stalking her. She studied his movements with fear in her eyes.

"Yeah, what do you have to say now?" Chauncey taunted her.

A gamut of emotions ran through Elisha as she just gaped at her ex with this crazed look in his eyes. The darkened glaze across his face matched the black clothing he wore. He looked like death.

"That's right, I saw you kissing him." He gave minia-ture rotations of a telling nod as if he had just caught her doing something she was forbidden to do. "You in your bathrobe and he's walking out like he's on cloud nine." Chauncey glared at her in disgust. "I thought he was never going to leave. And boy, those neighbors of yours still like to go out of town. You see, it wasn't hard to just park in their yard after seeing them pack up for one of those frequent getaways."

Elisha tried to run, but Chauncey grabbed her by the arm and wrapped his fingers around her throat. She clutched his wrist, desperately trying to free herself from his grip.

She gasped shallow breaths as Chauncey snatched her to the ground and pressed the side of her face against the cold, hard floor. Blood pumped rapidly through her veins as she grimaced from the pressure he applied.

"Now, we can do this the easy way or the hard way." His brows furrowed and danced a dangerous waltz.

"Please, Chauncey ... don't do this." Her voice crackled from the excess saliva in her throat.

He ignored her pleas, and confessed, "I'm glad I had somebody else to satisfy me when you wouldn't. And she didn't care that I had you as long as I had her back. It seems that a man with money has a lot of power these days. You can ask your friend Will about that."

Elisha's expression reflected the pain in her heart. She wanted nothing more than to be free from this man once and for all.

"And you never put two and two together that my father's last name is Gregory?"

Elisha wasn't sure if this crazed maniac really expected an answer from her or if he was simply being derisive towards her. So she just squeezed her eyes shut.

"That shows how much you really didn't care or just didn't listen to me. If you had, you would have known that I was back in town."

Elisha then remembered that his parents were never married and that Chauncey had his mother's maiden name since his father wasn't in his life until he was almost a teenager. She never gave the name Gregory a second thought when the news broke about the big real estate development project coming to town. Besides, he wasn't working for his father during the time they had dated.

"You should have known that I would be back." He clutched the back of her neck even harder. "I wouldn't just abandon ever seeing my family again, not even for you."

Elisha squeezed her eyes tighter and gasped for air.

Chauncey crumpled a portion of her robe into the palm of his other hand. "Welcome back to my world. Don't you know that I would have given you anything that you asked for if you just gave me a little something?" In all of his arrogance, he laughed at what his father's money had allowed him to get away with. He released the hold on Elisha's neck and she fought to catch her breath. Chauncey then flipped open her robe. "But right now, I'm going to get exactly what I deserve."

"That's one thing you got right." Tyler stood with a gun pressed against Chauncey's head. "Now get away from her with your hands on your head." Anger gripped Tyler's voice as he cocked the gun. "*Now!*"

Elisha scrambled from beneath Chauncey as he backed away from her. She quickly crawled into a corner and coughed violently. Tyler kept his gun aimed at Chauncey as he asked her, "Are you all right?"

"Ye-yes …" she finally answered, sobbing uncontrollably.

"Call 9-1-1," Tyler instructed her, and then turned his attention back to Chauncey. He kicked him in the stomach with all of the force he could muster. "How does it feel to be on the other side?" Tyler then stomped on him.

Chauncey groaned, twisting side to side in pain.

"Call them now, Elisha, before I kill this man!" Tyler kicked Chauncey again as he gripped the gun pointed at him even tighter.

Elisha dashed to the nearest phone and frantically dialed for help. Tears streamed down her face as she stared at Tyler's gun pointed directly at Chauncey. After crying into the phone what had just happened to a 9-1-1 operator, Elisha dropped the phone and struggled to control her breathing.

"Are you sure you're all right?" Tyler asked her again.

With a dazed look on her face, Elisha lunged at Chauncey and began pounding him in the face. She hit, clawed, and kicked his face, neck, and chest all the while screaming with each blow she landed. Tyler didn't try to stop her until after he heard the doorbell ring.

"Elisha!" Tyler pulled her by one hand off Chauncey. "Trust me, he's going to get exactly what he deserves." He steadied the gun in his other hand.

Elisha stumbled backward with tightened fists as the doorbell rang again.

"Get that or they're going to break your door down." Tyler tapped her arm and motioned for her to go. "I got this," he firmly said.

A disheveled mess, Elisha panted as she quickly backed out of the room into the hallway. For a brief moment, she glared at Chauncey who with drool on his lips groaned and rocked back and forth on the floor.

"Go!" Tyler shouted at her.

Elisha flinched out of her haze and ran to the front door. With shaky hands she flung the door open to find her mother promptly on the front steps.

"Why aren't you ready?" Margaret immediately started on her daughter as she walked inside. With a pair of crisp winter white dress pants on and square toe leather boots to match, she snatched each finger one by one of her gloves with the leopard print fur collar before she removed them completely.

"You know your sister. We have to get these things checked off the list before she comes home for a visit again." Margaret took a few more steps forward and gazed into the mirror on Elisha's wall. "Milton is only going to be in town for a week next month before he has to leave again. So, they trust us to take care of things. Not to mention that I told Francine and Kim to meet us in an hour." She fiddled with the curl in her bang before looking away from the mirror and at her diamond set Movado wristwatch.

Elisha stood motionless in the open doorway as her mother babbled incessantly. Margaret abruptly turned and faced her, only then did she see the horrid expression splashed across her daughter's face. "What's happened to you?" she questioned, now gaping at Elisha's hair and torn robe.

Elisha released a quivering breath just as a swarm of police cars squealed to a screeching halt on her lawn.

"What in the world?" Margaret gasped and dropped the gloves in her hands.

Three officers rushed up the front steps as Tyler emerged from around a corner, pushing Chauncey out in front of him. "Here he is! I caught him trying to assault my fiancée." Tyler flashed his badge that he always kept on him, and then pushed Chauncey off to another officer.

"Fiancée?" Margaret squinted as her eyes shifted from Tyler's to Elisha's. "Will somebody please tell me what is going on here?"

"Tyler, please tell them what happened," Elisha quickly said as Chauncey was detained.

In a panic, Margaret stared at Elisha's ripped bathrobe again. "What did he do?" The very life appeared to drain from her face.

Elisha hastily tightened the belt to the pink robe around her body. "Mama, come with me." She grabbed her mother's hand and pulled her to the back of the house.

Once inside of her walk-in closet, Elisha hugged her mother and began crying again.

"Elisha …" Margaret carefully held her daughter's head and stared into her eyes, still wearing the ghastly expression. "*What did he do?*"

Elisha sniffled as she tried to calm herself down. "He didn't do anything." She shook her head and placed her hands atop Margaret's on either side of her head. "Thank God, Mama, he didn't get a chance to."

Margaret closed her eyes and the color returned to her fair skin. "So, you're all right?"

"Yes." Elisha nodded. "But Mama, I've got to tell you something."

"What is it?"

Everything she had disclosed to Tyler about the abuse suffered at Chauncey's hands, Elisha shared with Margaret. The graphic pictures from the previous assault triggered tears from Margaret as she cupped her hands over her mouth and looked away. The mere thought that a man had beaten her daughter to a bloody pulp was more than she could bear.

After Margaret composed herself, she hugged Elisha tightly and sorely apologized for what she had gone through.

"Mama, this is not your fault. Both you and Daddy warned me about guys like him my whole life. I … I just couldn't bring myself to tell anybody because I was so ashamed." Tears streamed from Elisha's reddened, puffy eyes. "But I prayed for him to get caught." She sniffled between her words. "And who knows what would have happened if it wasn't for Tyler."

Margaret nodded knowingly as her husband Gerald had explained that Tyler had phoned him. Although he hadn't given her all of the details of that call, when Tyler called Elisha his fiancée it was easy to fill in the blanks.

"How can I ever face that man?" Margaret questioned herself. "Here, I've accused him of being a rapist when he's stopped one from raping my own daughter." She cleared the tears from beneath her own eyes by subtle strokes of her finger.

"Mama, it's okay now. Tyler is a good man. Look at how I had treated him. He was my best friend, but I sided with you not knowing the full story myself. But ..." She looked down, and then peered back up into Margaret's waiting eyes. "But now he's asked me to marry him ... *He wants me to be his wife.*" Elisha smiled through her tears, looking as if she was still trying to get used to the idea herself. "Just do what I did. Ask him for forgiveness."

Just then there was a knock at the closet door. "Elisha, is everything all right?" Tyler asked.

Elisha nodded, although she knew he couldn't see her, and responded, "Yes."

"Okay, well, the officers here need to take your statement."

"I'll be right out," she answered, and then looked at her mother with a wide, euphoric gaze. "Mama, I love him and he loves me. I've found my Mr. Right."

"I hear you." Margaret nodded and lovingly held the sides of her daughter's face again. "But from what your father was telling me, he found you first."

Chapter Twenty

Elisha hurried up the steps to her parents' home as she vigorously rubbed her gloved hands together. The spiral curls of hair bounced on her shoulders just beneath the white fitted beanie as she moved about, trying to keep warm. She glanced back across the frosted lawn as Tyler grabbed a covered dish from the back seat and motioned him on. After she pressed the doorbell for the third consecutive time, Gerald quickly opened the door.

"Hey, Daddy," Elisha said, her breath frosted in the air. She kissed her father on the cheek and quickly walked past him. "Brrr, it's cold out there." She briskly rubbed the sides of her arms. "It was just seventy degrees yesterday."

"Well, you know our Mississippi weather," Gerald quipped.

"Yeah, I know." Elisha glanced back at the vehicle in the driveway. "Tyler is just getting the dish from the back seat." She turned back to her father and asked, "Where's Mama?"

"In the kitchen," Gerald answered her with a broad grin.

"Okay." Elisha smiled back at him and disappeared to the kitchen.

Gerald stared outside and soon made room for Tyler to enter as he watched him walk up the steps to the front porch. "Hey, let me help you with that," Gerald offered as he reached for the oval-shaped container in Tyler's hands. "I see that Elisha cooked a little something." Gerald raised a brow.

Tyler closed the door behind them and shook his head. "Well, sir, I actually made this," he replied while pulling off his black toboggan hat.

"Oh, you made this," he clarified, almost as if he was relieved that his daughter hadn't tried her hand at baking since the last dish she brought over to the house. "I didn't know you cooked."

"Yes, sir. I've cooked for Elisha on many occasions." Tyler removed his heavy leather coat. "In fact, that right there is one of my favorite dishes."

"It smells like mine too." Gerald sniffed above the foil lined glass dish, and then met Tyler's waiting eyes. "*Dessert.*"

Both Tyler and Gerald shared a hearty laugh as they stood in the foyer.

"What are you two out here laughing about? Elisha and I are starving." Margaret smiled as she opened her arms to Tyler. "Hey, it's good to see you."

"Look honey … dessert. And Tyler made it." Gerald seemed proud as he extended the dish in his wife's direction.

"Oh, thank you Tyler, but you know you didn't have to bring anything."

"It's just a little something. Elisha told me how much you both like apple pie—"

"Yes, we really enjoy apple pie," Gerald chimed in with a wink.

"Well, this is just my spin on it."

"Your spin?" Margaret questioned.

"Yes, mine is just a healthier version. With a few minor substitutions, you barely know the difference," he explained.

"Substitutions?" Gerald grimaced.

"I think that sounds wonderful, Tyler," Margaret said and then turned to her husband. "I think your doctor will like the sound of that."

"Well, maybe he'll feel even better if I don't have dessert at all." Gerald handed the dish to Margaret.

"Come on, Mr. Maxwell. Once you try it, you won't even know the difference." Tyler patted his future father-in-law on the shoulder as he followed both him and Margaret into the dining room.

"Ask Margaret how many times she has said that to me," he said with a stone-face. His expression soon transformed into a telling smile as he answered for his wife, "Too many."

"Oh Gerald, you are too much." Margaret chuckled at her husband.

Elisha looked up from the small saucer of hors d'oeuvres as they all entered the room.

"Elisha, now I know you're not eating before we say a prayer." Margaret folded her arms across her chest.

"I prayed over my food," she said, feeding crumbs back into her mouth.

"It's my fault," Tyler admitted. "I had her out a little longer than expected and we didn't have time to eat. And since we were having dinner here, we didn't want to ruin our appetites so we came right over without even a bite to eat."

"Yeah, but he had me out with good reason." Elisha giggled and abandoned the remaining food on her saucer. "My ring came back today." She held up her left hand and wiggled her fingers.

"Oh honey, that is beautiful!" Margaret raved as she gazed at the ring on her daughter's finger.

Elisha winked at Tyler, signaling to him that he had done well if even her mother approved.

"He had to have it sized and engraved." Elisha, in all of her giddiness, removed the two-carat diamond cluster ring and handed it to her mother.

Margaret shared the view with her husband as they gazed at the inscription which read: *My one true love.*

"Aw, isn't that sweet." Margaret rested her head against Gerald's chest, and then gazed up into his eyes. "This reminds me so much of us."

"Yes, it does," Gerald agreed, recalling that they were childhood sweethearts.

"See, I told you," Elisha whispered to Tyler.

He nodded in response and whispered back, "Yeah, you did. She has really accepted me."

"There's no other way." Elisha gently slipped her hand in his.

Margaret handed the ring back to Elisha, and Tyler placed it back onto her finger where it belonged. The couples soon gathered around in a circle and held hands for a heart-warming prayer. As head of the household, Gerald offered thanksgiving to the Lord for the meal they were about to receive.

Moments like this gave him great pleasure to share in the committed love of one of his children. This would be his and Margaret's fourth child to announce an upcoming nuptial. His two sons were already married and playing professional football, his middle daughter, Charity, was recently engaged and due to get married in a couple of months, and now Elisha. He and Margaret shared another daughter, Joy, who was a senior in high school off with her best friend for the weekend. Marriage was the farthest thing from her mind and that's the way Gerald wanted to keep it, at least until after she graduated college.

"I'm starved," Gerald announced. "Let's eat."

"Amen to that, Daddy." Elisha made a beeline to the dinner table in the dining room while Tyler and Gerald washed up at the kitchen sink.

Moments later the four sat down to a meal fit for a king. Margaret went all out on the main course, prime roast, and the country fixings' like it was Thanksgiving or Christmas again. She enjoyed preparing a hearty feast, no matter what time of the year it was. And ever since she resigned from her job at the county office, Margaret had started her own interior design company and secured a few clients. The beauty of it was that she still had time for Joy and arranged her own schedule to keep a healthy balance between work and family. Although she planned to keep her state license active and up to date, her days of being a five day a week practicing attorney were over. And now that her husband was on break from touring the country, things were just the way she wanted them to be, calm, peaceful, and controlled.

"Mama, I'll never get tired of your macaroni and cheese. It tastes so good."

"Thank you. You know Charity has that on the menu for her reception."

Elisha's eyes suddenly lit up like a Christmas tree. "Mama, I just thought of something. Oh Tyler, you too, just let me know what you think." Her face practically glowed.

"Oh Gerald, I smell an epiphany coming on." Margaret leaned in and chuckled alongside her husband.

"No really, what do you guys think about a double wedding?"

Tyler paused, and then casually shrugged a shoulder. "A double wedding, huh?" He seemed to be tossing the idea around in his mind. "I'm okay with it."

"That might not be a bad idea," Margaret said, appreciating the thought that she would only have to oversee the catering of one event, but still enjoy the pleasure of being mother of two brides.

"Well, I don't have a problem with it either." Gerald nodded at his wife. "If Charity is on board, then—"

"Hey, Charity." Elisha had already dialed her sister's number and spilled the details into the waiting ear of her younger sister before Gerald could finish his sentence. "Can you believe it?"

The entire room could hear Charity screaming from the news her sister had just delivered. Elisha hadn't told anyone other than her parents and Tyler's mother that she was getting married. She wanted to wait until she had the ring on her finger because she knew that would be a question everyone would ask. Now that the ring was in place, Elisha was free to tell and show the whole world.

Charity stated that she would have to call Milton first, but was certain he wouldn't have a problem with the arrangement. Less than five minutes later, Charity phoned back and it was as expected, her fiancé was on board too with the idea of a double wedding.

On a whim, Charity volunteered her graphics expertise to design and send out invitations on Elisha's behalf to the same mailing list she had just weeks ago. With dinner on the table and a ravenous father waiting with folded arms who hated phones at the dinner table, they both decided to discuss additional invitees later.

"Okay, Daddy, I'm off the phone." Elisha cheerfully slid her phone towards the middle of the table away from her and scrunched her shoulders up to her ears. "Wow, I'm getting married in two months," she said with a radiant glow on her face. "Who would've thought?"

"Don't you mean *we're* getting married in a couple of months?" Tyler dotingly reminded her.

"Oh, you know what I mean." She playfully nudged his arm with her elbow.

Gerald smiled to himself. He glanced at his wife who wore a similar expression and raised a forkful of food to his mouth.

Elisha pecked Tyler on the cheek, elated even though their initial plans of eloping to Cape Cod had been changed by the unfolding of a dramatic event. Tyler had shown her that he was indeed spontaneously romantic ... at least when it came to her. On a moment's notice, he was prepared to marry Elisha and take her to the one place she said she wanted to go on her honeymoon. It would've cost him a pretty penny on such short notice, but Tyler justified that he only planned to get married once.

After dinner, Gerald and Tyler retired to the living room while Elisha and Margaret cleared the table at their urging. Elisha knew her father wanted to talk to Tyler some more, just as he had with Milton a month and a half prior. It was a new tradition that Gerald had started since this would be the first time he'd be giving his daughters away in marriage.

"So Tyler, what are your plans?"

"My plans, sir?" He quietly cleared his throat.

"Yes, where do you plan to live? Since you've moved to Tennessee and Elisha is here, what are your plans as far as a long-term residence?"

"Oh right … well, I've been thinking, *we've* been thinking, about making Lewiston our permanent home. At least for now."

Gerald's lips spread into a broad smile. When he had this similar talk with Milton, it was like music to Gerald's ears that he and Charity had made the same decision. It was something about having his girls close to home, especially since he traveled abroad so often. The fact that he had taken time off until Joy graduated high school ensured that there wouldn't be any schedule conflicts for him during the upcoming nuptials.

"Things are going well with me in Memphis, but my buddy, Nathan, has made it abundantly clear that all I have to say is a word and the chief would welcome me back with open arms at the precinct here. With more businesses moving to the area and the town growing fast, I think there'll be more than enough work to keep me busy. New money in a town can bring out the crazy in some people. Just look at what Elisha just went through."

Gerald nodded as Tyler mentioned the likes of Chauncey McDaniel. "I'm glad that you were there for her. That was quick thinking to ease in through her bathroom window."

"It was my police training," Tyler admitted. The layout of Elisha's house had been forever etched in his mind since the guided tour she had given him.

"And with all of the evidence stacked against him, the new DA assured us that he's going away for a while. Especially since Elisha had thought to have hidden cameras installed after what he had done to her before." Misty-eyed, Gerald fought back the looming anger that grew in the pit of his stomach. "If only she had said something before."

"I know." Tyler shared Gerald's sentiments. "But those cameras captured everything, so she was smart about it." He was also glad that the cameras were only in common areas like the kitchen, living room, and foyer. Although Chauncey had broken in and attacked Elisha, the defense attorney may have had a field day with seeing

Tyler and Elisha kicking Chauncey in the bedroom once he had already been subdued.

"And that's something I can live with."

"Me too," Tyler concurred.

The two men soon dismissed the topic of Chauncey all together. He was never going to hurt Elisha, or any other woman, again.

"Tyler, I want you to know that after you marry my daughter, you can still come to me. Man to man. I'll admit that I'm a little partial because she is my child, but I'm fair. We'll never have a problem as long as you are governing your household by the Good Book."

"I understand."

"As long as you never lay a hand on her—"

"Oh sir, you know I'd never do that." Tyler frowned.

"Hear me out," Gerald insisted. "And I'm sure you never will, but just let me say this."

Tyler released a slow breath. "Yes, sir."

"As long as you never lay a hand on her or call her out her name, we're good." Gerald steadied his eyes into Tyler's, driving his point home. "I'm telling you this not because I think you will treat her badly. Frankly, if I felt that way, I wouldn't have given you my blessing to marry her."

Tyler listened intently.

"If you have children, you may have to have this very same conversation with another young man. Don't get wrapped up in the right now so much that you can't see the bigger picture. You get me?"

Tyler was beginning to see what Gerald was saying. This man had seen him grow from an impressionable boy into an honorable man. Gerald had seen the highlights and low points of his life. It was only at that moment Tyler considered an opportunity like that may not exist for him to watch over the potential mates of his and Elisha's children. They had grown up in a town where everyone practically knew everyone, but now the city was changing. It was growing rapidly and more people were moving to the area. The small country town they once knew would soon be no more and Gerald challenged him to broaden his vision. He encouraged Tyler to not only to think as a husband, but as a father as well.

Gerald shared with Tyler the conversation he had with his mother when he visited her before she was released from the hospital. Gerald explained how she thanked him for being a positive role model in her son's life during his formidable teenage years. He reminded Tyler in no uncertain terms that although his father took off and left when he was a child, he was not fatherless.

"Always remember, God allowed me to come into your life, but even when I can't be there, *the Father* always is."

"Is he giving you the father speech?" Elisha joked, walking in having only heard the latter part of the conversation.

"No … he was giving me some good *Fatherly* advice." Tyler pointed above.

Gerald winked as he aimed a finger at Tyler. "You got it, son."

"Okay, I stand corrected." Elisha apologized with raised hands, and then chuckled. "I just came in to let you both know that dessert is ready. Would you like it in here or the kitchen with me and Mama?" She looked between the two of them.

"In here," they both responded in unison.

"*Okay*, I'll try not to take that personal." She smirked. "A couple of trays coming right up."

"Oh, Elisha." Gerald pulled her back by the deepness of his voice.

"Yeah, Daddy?"

"Bring me a cup of decaf coffee too. Black."

"Okay … be right back." Elisha started to walk away and stopped in her tracks. She turned around and leaned over Tyler's shoulder. "Would you like something to drink?"

Tyler smiled at her and nodded. "I'll have the same."

"No problem. Be right back." She kissed him on the cheek and then patted her father on the shoulder as she left the room.

Tyler looked at Gerald and they shared a telling grin.

"That was a teachable moment and my daughter picked up on it."

"Gotcha."

"So, are you ready for March Madness?" Gerald drew Tyler into the world of sports where they stayed for nearly an hour before Elisha and Margaret rejoined them.

There was so much to discuss, so many details to attend to, and so many loose ends to tie up before the spring event. An event Elisha had been waiting on for a long time. She had set out to find Mr. Right, but her search was over before it had begun. She just never realized that the man she wanted was being groomed right before her very eyes.

They had watched each other grow and be shaped into the people they each had prayed for. She wanted a protector, someone who would look out for her physically as well as spiritually. He wanted someone who would honor and respect him. Most importantly, they both desired a spouse who had dedicated their lives to Jesus Christ.

And tonight as they shared laughter, anecdotes of hope, and pearls of wisdom, the desires of their hearts were realized.

Delight yourself also in the LORD,
and He shall give you the desires of your heart.
~Psalm 37:4

About the Author

RENEE MCCOY (known to readers as Renée Allen McCoy) is a loving wife and mother, an author, but most importantly a devoted Christian. Having traveled to many parts of the world, today she, her husband, and their two children make Mississippi home. She maintains a newsletter, *Straight Up*, and a devotional blog, *In His Name*.

To date, she has penned eight books that include: The Fiery Furnace series (*The Kiss of Judas*, *Confessions*, and *The Eleventh Hour*), *Soul Ties: Breaking Up with a Past That's Killing Your Future* (A Non-fiction Title), *The Christmas Beau* (The True Love Novellas, Book 1), *In the Presence of My Enemies, Single, Saved, & Searching* (The True Love Novellas, Book 2), and *Once Upon a Sunday* (An Inspirational Short Story). Renée has also written for the world renowned pocket devotional, *The Upper Room*, both in digital and print.

With a heart to tell stories that will not only entertain, Renée hopes to enlighten readers to capture the message and power of God's saving grace.

Feel free to visit her online at www.ReneeAllenMccoy.com for more information on her forthcoming release, *A Test of Faith* (The True Love Novellas, Book 3).

FaytheWorks is an independent Christian publishing company that produces fiction and non-fiction titles. Since its formation, the goal has been and will always remain to share Christ focused stories and testimonies with the world. With a solid foundation on the Holy Bible, the infallible Word of God, we believe that Jesus Christ is Lord.

www.ingramcontent.com/pod-product-compliance
Lightning Source LLC
Chambersburg PA
CBHW020615250626
47154CB00004B/1520

* 9 7 8 0 9 8 3 6 0 4 6 5 5 *